C.-F. Ramuz

WHEN THE MOUNTAIN FELL

Pantheon Books

BY THE SAME AUTHOR

THE END OF ALL MEN

Manufactured in the U. S. A.
by H. Wolff, New York, N. Y.

ORIGINAL FRENCH TITLE
DERBORENCE
ENGLISH TRANSLATION BY
SARAH FISHER SCOTT

FIRST PART

1

A shepherd, missing, and
presumed dead, spent sev-
eral months buried in his
cabin, living on bread and
cheese. . . .

OLD ATLAS

IN HIS right hand he held a long stick, blackened at one end, and with this, from time to time,
he stirred the fire.

It was the twenty-second of June, near nine
o'clock in the evening.

Sparks flew up from under his stick, and clung
for an instant to the soot-blackened wall.

He could be seen more clearly when, for a
moment, he paused in his fire-tending, sitting
hunched over on the fireside bench. And opposite

9

him his companion—a much younger man—sitting also with elbows on knees, his head thrust forward.

"Well, then," said Seraphin—that is the older of the two—"I can see it all right . . . you're lonesome."

He looked across the fireplace and began to smile into his little white beard. "Just the same, it isn't as long as all that since we came up!"

They had come up around the fifteenth of June with the men from Aire and one or two families from the neighboring village of Premier.

Seraphin went back to his fire-tending. He threw fresh pine boughs on the fire, and as he stirred the coals the pine boughs blazed up so that now the two men could be seen again, sitting facing each other on opposite sides of the fire, each on the end of his bench: one already old, wizened but still tall, his small light eyes with no eyebrows sunk deeply in his head; the other very much younger, perhaps twenty to twenty-five, with white shirt and brown vest, a little black mustache and short black hair.

"Now look," said Seraphin. "Are you at the other end of the world? Are you now? Anybody would think you were never going to see her again. . . ."

He nodded his head once, and fell silent.

The point was that Antoine had been married only two months, and it's important to realize right away that the marriage hadn't taken place without difficulty. Orphaned early, Antoine at thirteen had been placed as a servant to work for a village family. On the other hand, the one he loved was well off. And for a long time her mother would hear no word in favor of a son-in-law who couldn't bring his fair share into the family. For a long time old Philomene was as obstinate as a mule, and she kept shaking her head, saying flatly, "No!" and then, "No!" and again "No!" Antoine and Therese could no longer meet except in secret.

And what would have happened if Seraphin hadn't been there? There—that is just in the right place, and important in that place too? For he was the brother of Philomene, the widow Maye, and, being a bachelor himself, he helped manage all her affairs. Seraphin had been on Antoine's side and had finally won out.

They were married in April, and now Seraphin and Antoine were on the mountain, as the saying goes.

At Aire it's the custom to come up to the mountain pastures around the fifteenth of June, villagers and animals together. Derborence, where they were that evening, was one of those pastures, and

Seraphin had brought Antoine along to teach him the work because he himself wasn't getting any younger. He limped, he had a stiff knee. And now that rheumatism had attacked his left arm, he ran a risk some fine day of being unable to use it at all—no small inconvenience in those mountain cabins where the cows have to be milked morning and evening, and the butter and cheese made once a day without fail. So Seraphin had brought Antoine along with him, hoping that he would be able to take his place before long. But it looked now as if Antoine wasn't going to work into it. The work was new and, far from his wife, he was getting dull and bored.

"Look," Seraphin said again, "aren't things going any better? After all, is it such an awful thing to have me for company?"

He had no thought for himself, he thought only of Antoine. It was to Antoine that Seraphin was speaking, that evening of the twenty-second of June, near nine o'clock in the evening. And since the fire was dying down, he fed it again and brought it back to life with some pine branches.

"Why no, of course not," said Antoine.

That was all, he held his peace. And since Seraphin was no longer speaking either, around the two men there slowly grew a strange thing, inhuman, and in the end unbearable—Silence. A

silence of the high mountains, a silence of un-
peopled spaces, where man comes but rarely, and
where, if by chance he falls silent himself, he may
listen all he will, but all that he can hear is that
there is nothing to hear.

It is as if nothing exists any more anywhere,
from us to the other end of the world, from us to
the furthest reach of the sky. Nothing, the abyss,
the void; the annihilation of self; as if the world
were not yet created, or had ceased to exist; as if
it was before the beginning of the world, or after
its end. And anguish dwells in your throat, and a
hand is slowly contracting around your heart.

A lucky chance if just then the fire starts to
crackle, or a drop of water falls, or perhaps a little wind brushes the roof. The slightest little
sound is a great sound. The drop of water rever-
berates as it falls. The burning wood cracks like
a pistol shot, and the brushing of the wind is
enough all by itself to fill the immensity of space.
All the tiny sounds that are really loud . . . they
recur . . . they fill the cup of silence. Life begins
again because of the living sounds.

"Now look. After all . . ." Seraphin began
again.

The fire was still crackling.

"Besides," he went on, "if you want to go down

Saturday . . . you could stay there two or three days and spend Sunday with her. . . ."

"And you?"

"Oh, me! As for me," said Seraphin, "I'm used to it. Don't you worry about me."

He began to smile again into his beard, that beard which had almost turned white while his mustache was still black. It was near nine o'clock in the evening, the twenty-second of June, in the mountain cabin where the two men were sitting near the fire.

From time to time, on the roof, something went "Crack!"

And Seraphin went on, "You can come back when you feel like it, I'll get along all right. And then," he said, "when you come back, you won't be all alone here."

He smiled into his white beard, looking steadily at Antoine with his little gray eyes.

"Or do I count for nothing?"

"Oh, no!" said Antoine.

Something cracked again on the roof, made of beams and heavy slabs of rock, which rose steeply over their heads and had but one pitch, since the cabin was backed up against the ledge of rock which formed its fourth wall.

"Then it's settled for Saturday. That's only three days away . . ."

"Many thanks."

Something cracked. The slates, lying out all day exposed to the sun, had expanded in the heat, and now, with the return of evening and the mountain cold, were contracting again, making sudden sounds with long intervals in between, as if someone were walking on the roof. One step cautiously advanced, then a long pause, just as a thief would pause before risking himself any further, to make sure that he had not been heard. It cracked, then cracked no longer; in the sudden quiet they saw each other, then saw each other no longer. It was the fire flaming up, it was the fire dying down again.

But Antoine lifted his head: a new sound had just made itself heard. An entirely different sound, this time, a sound both loud and totally unexpected, a sound which seemed to come from the end of space. It was like the rolling of thunder, beginning with a sharp report; and now, although still reverberating, it was all broken up by new crashes, themselves prolonged by their own echoes.

"Ah!" said Seraphin, "so they're beginning again. . . ."

"Who, they?"

"What? You haven't heard anything, these past nights? And a good thing too, but then you're a heavy sleeper. Besides," Seraphin went on, "you haven't got the feel of it around here yet. Well, up here—all you need to do is to remember the name of the mountain . . . yes, the peak where the glacier is. Come on, don't you know it . . . ? The Devil's Tower. . . ."

The sound was dying, little by little, and was now very soft, almost imperceptible, like that of a little wind which runs through a thicket, barely moving the leaves.

"Just the same, you surely remember the story. Oh well, then, that HE lives up there, with his wife and children."

There was now no sound at all in the night.

"And then, at times, he gets bored and says to his imps: 'Get out the bowls!' It's up there where the Nine Pin is—you know the place—exactly: The Devil's Pin, and it's a game they've got. They aim at the pin with their balls. And good-looking ones too, I tell you! All made out of precious stones. They're blue, they're green, they're transparent. . . . Only sometimes, you see, they miss the pin, and it isn't hard to guess where their ammunition goes then. What is there off the edge of the glacier? Nothing. It's the end. Nowhere to go but down. Sometimes you can see them falling when there's a full moon, and just now there's a full moon. . . ."

He said, "Do you want to come and see?"

Was Antoine uneasy? You couldn't tell. But he was certainly curious, and when Seraphin stood up, he did too. Seraphin went ahead. He opened the door. Just as he had said, the night was flooded with moonlight, laying a brilliant white square of light on the floor of beaten earth behind them.

It was a grassy valley, flat, dotted with a few cabins. It was like a meadow, but a meadow narrowly fenced in by the rocks piled up into haphazard walls. As the two men faced south, they could see where the moon had risen behind a jagged jumble of peaks, at the foot of which they stood. Then, turning toward the west, they could see the walls beginning, not very high at first, and continuing on in a mounting half-circle to the north and east.

Seraphin lifted his arm. His hand was visible in the soft light, the forefinger pointing and nearly straight up over his head. You would have to tip your own head way back to follow it. Seraphin was pointing out something up there, four thousand feet overhead.

And now it was easy to see that on that side too —on the north—they were completely shut in, and on the west as well, where the pass was screened by the first buttress of the mountain.

Seraphin raised his arm again, conjuring up a new wall higher than any of the others, and they could see that they were surrounded. It was as if they were standing at the bottom of a well, except that the steep walls were fissured from top to bottom by narrow gorges, each with its tiny waterfall hanging in a wavering white line. Their gaze swept evenly around the rim, then halted where Seraphin's forefinger still pointed at the sky.

It was up there, right on the edge of the parapet at its highest point. Just there the rock jutted out into space, and towering along its whole width was the rim of the glacier. Something up there was shining softly: a luminous fringe, faintly transparent, with gleams of blue and green and a sheen like phosphorescence—it was the broken edge of the ice, and in that enchanted hour of the night it too was filled with infinite silence and infinite peace. Nothing stirred anywhere under the impalpable white down of moonlight which seemed to drift effortlessly on the night air and settle in thin sheets on every smooth surface.

"Up there."

Seraphin was still pointing.

"Yes, right up there where it hangs over. But it looks as though it's all finished for tonight."

His voice rang out loudly in the silence.

"Yes," he went on, "it's been going on like that as far back as anyone can remember."

He lowered his arm.

"The old people speak of its happening in their time. And they were still little children when they heard their own grandparents telling about it. The only thing is, it's chancy. Too bad. . . ."

From time to time they could hear the tinkle of a goat bell somewhere near-by. The little cabins were scattered here and there over the valley. Their little dry-stone walls were low and sturdy, and on one side their roofs were all snowed under with moonlight; the other, velvet black, melted into its own shadow on the ground.

The two men waited a moment longer to see if anything was going to happen; but what went on happening was still nothing at all.

At the most, from time to time a faint breath of air brought to their ears the distant whisper of a waterfall. The breath of air itself was like a hand smoothing down the earth, as it ran along close to the ground. Everything slept: the men in their cabins, the animals in their stables and on the moonlit pasture.

And up there . . .

Up there, where they were still looking, there was only that slender rim of ice gleaming in the moonlight, so fragile, so tenuous, that from mo-

19

ment to moment it seemed to waver like a thread lifted by a little breeze. Antoine thought he could see it move. He was even going to speak about it, but Seraphin began to shake his head.

"Looks as if the devil's gone to bed; how about our doing the same?"

So Antoine said nothing. The two men went back into the cabin and pulled the door to behind them.

Their beds were straw mattresses laid on rough boards built into the wall like bunks, so that they slept one above the other, as if they were in a ship.

Antoine slept on the upper bunk.

They hung their shoes by the laces from a peg, because of the rats.

Antoine climbed up.

"Good night," said Seraphin.

And he answered:

"Good night."

And there she was, right away she was with him, as soon as he had rolled up in his brown wool blanket and turned toward the wall. Why weren't things going well? Because of Therese.

She came back and was sitting there, somehow finding room for herself and the fields around her in the narrow strip of space between him and the wall. He said, "hello"; she said, "hello." He said, "Well, now . . . ," she said, "You see, it's like this." They had to meet far from the village, because there were always busybodies around. There are always busybodies, always people who want to stick their noses into what is none of their business. She had a rake on her shoulder; he could see how the teeth of the rake caught on the clouds as they sailed by. The clouds were falling on his head. Why had he sat down above her on the bank? All he could see was her back, and she was bending forward so that she showed a little patch of sun-browned skin between her knot of hair and her red kerchief.

"What's the matter?"

"Oh," she said, "it's not me."

"Well, what is it?"

"Oh," she said, "it's my mother."

Things hadn't gone well in those days either.

She began to slide. He said, "Wait for me." She slid faster and faster, still sitting quietly without moving at all. It was as if the ground was slipping away from under her; and she flew more and more rapidly on in front of him, but he was flying too: they were still the same distance apart and could talk to each other. Everything was going fast. He was saying, "The only thing is, you know, look out for the Rhône!" Because the Rhône was at the foot of the mountain. And it isn't winter, either, he thought to himself.

"My mother said, just like that, that if we had children there wouldn't be enough to live on."

Look out!

There was a crash—was he still sleeping?

The queer noise he thought he had heard was still going on.

Was it just inside his head? There was a noise like water in his ears—he was asleep—was he asleep? He turned over, he saw that the door to the cabin was opening: somebody was cautiously leaning in through the doorway, half lit by the moonlight which stopped in a straight white line across his back.

Where is she?

"Well now," he said to himself. "Things have straightened out since then, haven't they? Sure, sure, we're married now, it's all settled; that was the old days. . . ."

He thought, "Saturday. . . ."

He opened his eyes; the cabin was deserted again and the square of moonlight in front of the door was blank and empty, like an artist's canvas on which there is as yet no picture.

He had gone back to sleep—had he gone back to sleep?

But all at once the roof fell in, and one of the beams, snapping off at one end, came crashing up against the bunk where Antoine lay.

2

Derborence—the word itself has a singing sound, it rings softly and a little sadly inside your head. It begins sharply and decisively, then hesitates, becomes undecided, and trails away while you are still saying it. Derborence. Finally it breaks off suddenly as if to symbolize by its own sound neglect, isolation, ruin.

For devastation reigns over it now, no flock climbs there for pasture, man himself has turned away from it. It is five or six hours away from the plain, that is if you come from the west, the Vaud country. Derborence, where is it? People tell you, "It's over there in back." You have to climb a long time, following up a stream of mountain water, so clear it looks like air flowing over the stones of its bed. Derborence lies between two long, irregular mountain ranges, and the path climbs up between them for a long way. They are like two knife blades fixed in the earth, the sharp edge all jagged, showing at times the gleam of steel, but everywhere else eaten with rust. And they rise higher and higher on either hand. The more you climb, the higher they tower into the sky; and the name, Derborence, goes on singing gently in your head while you pass the well-built cabins of those parts, their long white walls neatly plastered, their roofs covered with slates looking like the scales on a fish. There are stables for the stock, there are gushing springs.

The path goes on climbing, the slope is steeper. All around are wide pastures sweeping down from one ledge of rock to another like stairs. You climb from one broad shelf to another. Already you are not far from Derborence; not far either from the country of the glaciers. And now at last there is a pass where the mountains close in again, and just here are the pastures and mountain cabins of Anzeindaz, like a little village, not far from where the grass itself can no longer grow. For a long time now there have been no trees.

Derborence is close by. All you have to do is to walk straight in front of you.

And suddenly the ground falls away from beneath your feet.

All at once the line of grass against the sky, which dips slightly in the middle, is outlining its hollow curve over nothingness itself. You have arrived. A chasm opens abruptly below you, like an immense oval basket with precipitous sides over which you have to lean, because although you are yourself six thousand feet up, the bottom is seventeen or eighteen hundred feet below you, straight down.

You bend over, you lean your head forward a little. Or else lie down flat, and look over the edge into the depths.

A breath of cold air blows into your face.

Derborence. It's first of all like a piece of winter blowing against you in full summer, for it is the home of shadows, which cling there even when the sun is highest in the sky. Then you can see that there is nothing there any more. Just stones, and more stones, and still more stones.

All around it the walls fall steeply, irregular in height, now rough, now smooth, while the path wriggles and twists down them far below like a snake. And whether you look straight ahead or on either side, there they are, standing on edge, lying on their sides, propped up or fallen flat, pushing forward in spurs from the mountain side or half-hidden and folded into narrow ravines—everywhere stones, nothing but stones, everywhere the same desolation.

Where the sunlight shines on them, they gleam with variegated color, but only a few of them, for one wall shadows the other, and the southern mountain cuts off most of the sun from that on the north. For a little while you can still see the top of the parapet all golden like a ripe grape, or red like a rose.

But the shadow is spreading already, it climbs higher and higher up the sides; it rises irresistibly and little by little like water in the bowl of a fountain, and as it rises everything fades, all is chill and silent, everything faints and dies; while everywhere the same sad color, the same bluish tint spreads below you like a fine mist through which you can see two lonely little lakes still gleaming a little longer like flat tin roofs in the gathering darkness. Then they, too, disappear.

The valley is still there, but nothing moves in it. You can look as long and as carefully as you will, everything is as still as death. Look: from the towering walls on the south to those on the north, nowhere is there any room for a living thing. There is nothing but the barren rock.

Once the valley was alive, now everything has been blotted out by something that seems at first glance like a cone of sand, with the narrow end still half held in the northern wall; and from there the rocks are scattered helter-skelter all over like dice from a dicebox, and that's exactly what they are like, dice of all sizes, one square block and another just like it, blocks piled up on top of each other, then a succession of blocks, big and little, choking the valley as far as the eye can see.

And yet many people used to come to the valley in the old days. They even say that some years there were as many as fifty.

They climbed up by way of the gorge whose river flows into the Rhône below. They came from Aire and from Premier—little villages of the Valais perched high on the north slope of the Rhône valley.

They moved out near the middle of June with their little brown cows and their goats, having built for their use many small cabins with dry-stone walls, roofed with slate, in which they lived for two or three months in the summer.

The pastures in those days were all a beautiful green color from the month of May on, for up there it is the month of May that brings the new colors of spring.

Up there (people say "up there" when they come from the Valais, but when they are from Anzeindaz they say "down yonder" or "over in the bottom") the snow as it shrinks leaves heaped-up drifts, and beside them, in the damp black earth, barely covered by the dull brown felt of the old grass, grow all kinds of little flowers, blooming right up to the edge of a sheet of ice thinner than window glass. All kinds of little mountain flowers with their extraordinary brilliance, their extraordinary purity, their extraordinary colors: whiter than the snow, bluer than the sky, bright orange, violet — crocuses, anemones, primroses. . . . From a distance they make brilliant splashes of color between the gray patches of the retreating snow. As if they were on a silk kerchief, one of those that the girls buy in town when they come down from the villages to the fair of Saint Pierre or Saint Joseph. Later it is the foundation color of the cloth itself which changes: the gray and white vanish, everything bursts into green, the sap rises, the grass comes back again. It is as if drops of green had fallen from a painter's brush and quickly, quickly had run together, each drop spreading and flowing to join the others.

How beautiful Derborence was in those days! Beautiful and joyous and welcoming, all ready with the coming of June for its people.

And they were only waiting for the sign of spring — they came.

One afternoon the monotonous roar of the torrent was pierced and broken up by the gay tinkle of a bell. First a single cow appeared, then ten, then fifteen, then as many as a hundred.

The little goatherd blew on his pipe.

They lit the fires in the cabins; everywhere above the chimneys or from the open doors graceful blue plumes of smoke swayed gently in the still air.

The plumes grew taller, they flattened out up above and mingled together. Soon they were like a transparent ceiling or a delicate spider web stretched across the valley halfway up the rocky walls.

And underneath life began and life went on: the scattered roofs seeming like little books on a green carpet, all the roofs bound in gray, two or three brooks gleaming here and there, like sunlight reflected from a sword blade; round specks, oval specks, some still, some moving, the round specks being men, the oval ones cows.

All that was long ago, when Derborence was still lived in, before the mountain fell.

But now . . . now it has just fallen.

3

W<small>HEN THE MEN</small> from Anzeindaz were telling
about it, they said,

"It began like a salvo of cannon—all six guns
in the battery firing at once.

"And then," they said, "there was a blast of
wind.

"After that more cannons, shots and explosions,
Bang! Crash! Bang! Crash! as if the mountain
were shooting at us from all sides.

"The wind flung the door wide open, as if somebody had burst in, and the ashes from the fireplace
began falling on us as if it were snowing in the
cabin.

"As for us, well, you know, there on the pass
we aren't far below the place where the landslide
broke off. We're just a little bit more on one side
and in back, and the first noise we heard was the
crash of the overhang when it hit bottom; after
that it was just war between one range and an-

other, one ridge and the other, one peak and the
other. It was like thunder around each of the
mountains which stand in a half circle there—
from the Argentine to the Morcles, from the Rocks
of the Wind to Saint Martin."

They were already on their feet. There were
three of them. They couldn't find their tinder.

The cows, which had been brought in for the
night but not tied up, were making a terrible
racket in the stable and threatening to knock
everything down.

First of all the men had to go and straighten
that out.

They had a horn lantern with them, although it
seemed foolish at first to take it in such brilliant
moonlight. But soon they were astonished to see a
gray shadow coming over the moon, which began
to look faded and bleak as it does when there is an
eclipse, while on the other hand the light from the
lantern shone brighter and brighter, casting a
circle of light on the short grass before their feet.

It was then that they saw the great pale cloud
rising before them. The silence was coming back
little by little, and in the quiet the cloud towered
higher and higher behind the ridge which still hid
the depths of Derborence; it was like a wall rising
above another wall. It was like a great pillar of
smoke, but flat, with no billows or curves; it was

32

like a bank of mist, but slower, heavier; and the whole mass grew from within toward the top, like bread rising when the dough is mixed and put in the bread trough, and it swells in the trough, and overflows the edges.

The men said to each other, "My God, what's that?"

They said, "It's dust."

They said, "The mountain has fallen."

They coughed, they sneezed, they bowed their heads, trying to shelter behind their hat brims.

But it was a fine powder, an impalpable dust and, since it floated everywhere in the air, it penetrated everything. In any case they had to plunge into it, for it was now coming toward them. They went forward a few steps, then a few more. They stopped. One of them even said, "Do you think it's safe to go any further?"

He said, "Is it solid underfoot, ahead there? Anyhow, it doesn't look as if we could see much."

But they were pushed ahead by pride; they were pushed ahead by curiosity.

Besides, the noises were becoming rarer and rarer, with longer intervals between them. They were duller and more internal, like intestinal rumblings inside the earth; so that the three men could move forward with more confidence to the edge of the abyss.

They could see nothing, nothing but this white moving mass. At times they saw nothing at all; at times there came a break or tear in the swirling clouds and they could see still more mist beyond, but the clouds themselves hid everything else. They hid not only the bottom of the valley, but the walls around it, so that the men could neither see where the avalanche had broken off, nor where it had landed — there was nothing but swirling fumes, as if they were looking into a steaming wash boiler, nothing but a vast confusion of vapors faintly lit and reddened by the moonlight. The moon was all red up there in the sky. First it disappeared in the streaming mist, then reappeared again.

The lantern on the ground beside the men paled, shone out strongly, paled again; they themselves were lying flat on the ground, their heads barely far enough over the edge to let them see.

And one of them said, "How many do you suppose they were?"

"Lord Jesus!"

The third said, "Have to know whether they'd all come up yet or not. . . . Fifteen, maybe. Twenty. . . ."

Although they still coughed from time to time, they were growing used by now to the lack of air, so they stayed there and began to talk in low tones.

From underneath them came muffled grumblings from deep in the earth; and since they were stretched out flat on the ground, each one could hear with his whole body the noises of the mountain, rising inside him to his ears.

The men from Sanetsch had hurried to the spot too. They came from the northwest, at the other end of the great wall of mountains, and were watching from a ledge above the Woodcutter's Passage, where it drives straight down to the bottom through narrow chimneys in the rock. They were talking to each other in their own dialect, unintelligible to most people, since it is derived from the German. They talked with many gestures. Nobody saw them. They couldn't even see each other. To get there, they had had to cross a whole section of boulders long ago worn and weathered by water and looking like a sea turned suddenly to stone, still showing its succession of crests and hollows and overhanging waves, and pierced with many potholes. They too stared questioningly into the depths, and heard no answer but unintelligible growls and meaningless grumblings; only those leaping tongues and swirls of dust.

They were caught in dust themselves, with a taste of crushed slate in their mouths; they were enveloped first in one thickness, then in another, swathed in folds of billowing dust, first covered, then uncovered a little, then swallowed up again.

As for the men of Zamperon, they stuck to their bunks until daybreak. There are just three or four cabins there where the people from Premier, the nearest village to Aire, spend the summer. Zamperon, its three or four cabins only a little below the valley of Derborence, where it opens out into the gorge that goes down to the Rhône. It was right in the path of the blast of wind when it burst out, snatched the slates from the roofs, blew two or three little shed roofs right off, tumbling them away like straw hats, flattened a grove of young saplings on a shoulder of the mountain, and passing through the cracks of the unmortared walls, struck at the men asleep inside, pinning them down in their beds.

They could hear the cheese buckets tumbling down, benches crashing to the floor, doors shaking as though someone were trying to burst them in. At one and the same time everything moved, everything rumbled. It crackled and whistled; the noise came out of the air, from the ground and underneath the earth in a terrible confusion of all the elements in which nobody could distinguish which was noise and which motion, nor what the noises meant, or where they came from, or where they were going to, as if it was the end of the world. And the men of Zamperon, flattened out in their beds and clutching the sides to keep from being thrown out, clung there more dead than alive. Motionless, without a sound, mouths open in fear but full of silence, with every part of their bodies shaken and emptied of life, they remained paralyzed for a long time. Little by little the air fell back into its accustomed calm, little by little nothing was to be heard but a few dull rumbles and distant crashes; they still said nothing, they did not begin to call to one another.

They had to wait until dawn, which luckily comes early at that time of year. Usually from half-past three on, a pale and uncertain light wavers and shifts in the sky above the rim of the eastern mountain, and the stars fall before it one by one, like ripened fruit from a tree. But on that day there was no mountain, there was no horizon, and no sun either.

When the daylight came, it spread sluggishly and with difficulty, appearing finally more or less all over without showing itself first at any particular spot. And when it did, all that it disclosed was a heavy yellow fog covering everything, astonishing the first man who came out, and in which he was astonished to find himself. There was something else surprising too, but at first he couldn't figure out what it was.

He was a man named Biollaz, from Premier.

Sitting up on his bed, after it first began to be light, he called to his partner, "You coming?"

No answer. He called again. "Loutre! Hey, Loutre!" Nothing. "Or maybe you're dead, huh?"

He could see the sky through a hole in the roof that the wind had torn open in the night. It was right over his head and big enough for a man to crawl through. And since there was still no answer, he put one leg out of bed, a trousered leg, for he had slept with his clothes on. Nothing, and still nothing. He swung his other leg out.

"Loutre?"

And now finally Loutre moved a little.

Biollaz saw Loutre lying in bed looking at him.

"Aren't you coming with me?"

The other shook his head.

"All right, I don't care. I'm going out anyway."

Biollaz stood up. It was not at all dark in the room, because of the hole in the roof, and he could move about without any trouble. Everything in the cabin was on the floor. The things which had been hung on pegs or laid on shelves had fallen off the pegs and the shelves. The milk pans were all knocked over.

He put his shoes on and walked through the puddles of milk to the door.

But the door was stuck—the wall had sagged and sprung the door frame.

Finally he had to go out through the hole in the roof.

Loutre helped push him up, holding his legs until he got through. Then he turned around and leaning through the hole, gave Loutre a hand up. Jumping down from the roof, he stood astonished at the fog and still more astonished at the great silence around him.

For something was missing, something which used to be there was there no longer; Biollaz tried to think what it could be and suddenly it came to him: it was the noise of the river which could no longer be heard, although it was the season of the year when the water was highest.

"Loutre, Loutre, where are you?"

"Over here."

"Loutre, can you hear? The Lizerne. . . ."

And then Loutre said, "I'm coming."

There were two of them then, and they walked down the path thickly strewn with the slabs of stone blown off the roofs. The slates had split as they fell, and showed a grain like wood.

People were coming out of the other houses.

From a distance they could barely see each

other. And even when they came close it was hard for a man to recognize his neighbors, because their faces were still pale and drawn from the night's terror. They hardly spoke at all: they sighed, they looked at each other, they shook their heads. As they came by the Donneloye house the door burst open. A boy stood on the stoop staring at them— but did he really see them? For without saying a word he suddenly started to run as hard as he could down the path to the valley. They called, "Hey, Dsozet!"; he heard nothing. They called, but he had already disappeared, swallowed up in the opaque fog which opened to let him through, then closed behind him like a heavy curtain.

They went on up the path that led to Derborence, only a quarter of an hour away. As they walked, they had to push through the strange fog which barred their way, hanging down like successive curtains of dingy cotton wool, or like the leaves of a book, held together at the top by the binding, but fanned out below. And little by little they were shredding away, there was more and more light visible through the mist, finally the men were able to see. They saw that the way was blocked. Across the path, straight up and down, was something like an enormous wall. It loomed up like a fortification, with its sloping approach, trenches, loopholes, and beetling outer wall. It was a wall, sure enough, and it must have come down in the night. But from where? They could not tell. But there it was, blocking the way with its big stones and little ones, its sand, gravel and rubble, while the river bed coming out from under it was all dried up, the bottom of its bed bare and rocky and showing only a few trapped pools of water.

"Stop!"

"Who's that?"

It was old Plon, the shepherd of the Dubonere. On their left a steep ravine cut through the mountain chain to the southwest, so rocky and arid that only sheep could graze there.

There his flock could be seen, tumbling down the rocky slopes and looking like a fall of stones itself.

Or in the bottom of a hollow, like a little lake with its surface ruffled by the wind.

Or wandering on the slopes like a cloud shadow.

They saw the flock, and in front of it was old Plon.

"Stop!"

He was perched on top of a big rock and held out his arm toward them.

"Don't go any further!"

He shook his head mysteriously. His white beard showed between the folds of his long cape. It was the color of rust, the color of moss, that cape, the color of bark or stone, it was the color of all outdoor things, having, like them, known sunshine, downpours, snow, cold, heat, wind, tempests, the quiet air and the long succession of days and nights.

"Don't go any further! D . . E . ."

He began to laugh.

"D . . E . . V . . D'you understand?"

And as he was talking, there in front of them something moved between the stones; somebody was trying to come toward them.

It was a man, but a man barely able to stand or walk; desperately clutching at the nearest rock before he dared take a step, then trying it anyway and falling over sideways in a heap.

They looked, and looked more closely.

"Good God!" they said, "it's Barthelemy!"

And they ran to meet him, while behind them they could hear old Plon calling:

"Look out! Don't go any further. . . . Stop! Stop!"

4

THAT EVENING Therese was sitting in front of her
house, where a board nailed on four stakes made
a bench close to the stone foundation. She sat
there in her full brown dress, cut to show the
rough linen sleeves of her blouse. She sat leaning
forward with her arms loosely on her knees, looking aimlessly below her over the low trees of the
orchard to the valley at the bottom of the great
slope which plunged away from her gaze in its
steep descent; to the valley and the plain — the
great paper-smooth plain far below, through
which flowed the Rhône.

"Lord! How time drags on . . . how everything
stays the same. Eight days since Antoine left, and
it seems like eight months!"

She sat relaxed, her head tipped forward, looking at the Rhône on the flat green plain. The
Rhône was gray and white, its bed much wider
than the river, because the sand and gravel carried

along by the current kept encroaching on its banks.

There in the valley, its path was as sharply marked as a road on a map. Its bed was all twisted and capricious with gray edges of alluvial mud. The river itself ran along in the middle, you could see it moving in the middle, clear gray, almost white, writhing down the valley like a snake.

There, too, everything was the same, there, too, nothing changed. Oh, she knew it well, the Rhône, too well!

All that time, she thought, all that time it's been mumbling the same old story (which you can hear any time you listen, which you can hear even better at night).

Maybe Antoine could come down Sunday—but he would just have to go back up again. Barely reunited, we'll be separated again; barely married, unmarried. If only Antoine could come home for good! And here I am, looking at the Rhône . . . as if there'd be time for that, with the two of us together!

I'm tired of it, I'm tired of it.

She could hear footsteps on the other side of the house. People were coming home for supper.

The day was over: it began at four o'clock in the morning and finished at eight in the evening.

They were coming home. She could hear the

sound of footsteps, now dull, now loud; muffled because of the mud underfoot and then ringing out clearly on the big flat stones laid down in the alley like steppingstones.

On that side of the village, the fronts of the houses were in two colors, white below, brown above: on the other, their backs were much lower and barely rose above the narrow alley between them and the next line of buildings. These, too, were black and white in front and neatly set in line like beehives in a garden, while at the back they were all black and straggled crookedly to darken the perpetually muddy back alley.

Nobody ever passed in front of the houses, but in the alley in back all the village came and went: women with their rakes over their shoulders, little girls with pails of water, but only one or two men, for it was a summer village; nearly all its men who were old or strong enough had gone up to the mountain. The only ones left were the aged or infirm, the simple ones, or those who had no cattle.

It was a lovely evening. At her feet she could see some little red ants in single file carrying their eggs along a tiny crack that they had managed to dig in the dust—like their village street, she thought, for the ants are like us; the ants with their eggs bigger than they are, like us with our bundles of hay bigger than we are. . . .

Suddenly she felt hot all over and the blood hummed in her ears. Even when she straightened up it was hard to breathe. She flushed red, then paled, then flushed again.

What was it?

She sat wondering; then suddenly an idea came to her — after all, she was married now. . . . She had been married for two months.

Could that be it?

Again she turned pale: oh, surely, that was it! Besides, what else could it be, since she was so healthy?

Surely that was it! And she flushed once more, she began to smile, her lips were again as red as her kerchief. She tipped her head back and leaned it against the wall, her heavy knot of hair forming a sort of pillow for her head.

It felt so good that she didn't move. "Because, if it's that . . . if it's that, I won't be alone any longer. There will be two of us while he is away, and when he comes down, we will be three. . . ."

In front of her and just on a level with her eyes the mountains soared into the sky. Not just one, or two, or ten, but hundreds of them, in a semi-circle, like a garland of flowers hanging low in the sky.

They were higher than the forests, higher than the pastures, higher than the rocks; there hung the snows, the gleaming icefields which seemed to float away from the earth—strangers to their own foundations already deep in the evening shadow. And the darker the shadow grew, the more they seemed to float in the air and the more they glowed with a light that was made of all the tones of rose and red and gold and silver.

Her heart felt soft and warm in her breast. When they were married in April, the peach trees were in bloom. Now they were blooming again, it was like a promise. She looked around the circle of mountains again, yes, they were like blossoming peach trees. They reminded her of the season when the wild roses bloom, or when the late and timid wild quinces open their buds last of all. Now the mountains began to pale and fade; they were turning gray, but what does it matter? she thought, tomorrow they will be in flower again.

There were no footsteps in the street any more. The women were calling their children. They came to the doorstep, called two or three times, then called once more. And Therese realized that she had forgotten the time. Her mother must be waiting for her, for she had been eating at her mother's house since Antoine left.

She started out quickly, going through the back gardens to avoid meeting anybody who might stop her and talk. She could see the door, a square of red light above the outside staircase. And she held on to the rail as she climbed, for she felt a little dizzy.

Somebody said, "Well, it's about time . . . where have you been?"

There was Philomene, a black silhouette against the fireplace with its hanging kettle, her head turned toward Therese and the door.

"Come on, come on, hurry and light up."

Therese took a twig of larch wood — that evening of the twenty-second of June, around half-past eight, while Seraphin and Antoine were sitting before the fire at Derborence. They were sitting by the fire, Seraphin and Antoine, and one by one the stars were coming out in the sky; the moon was going to rise. In all the big dark kitchen, there was only one glow of light; her mother was standing before it. Therese took the twig and carried it over to the fire — the twenty-second of June. She came back, holding the little trembling flame in her cupped hands, so that they glowed with light, and held it to the wick of the lamp hanging on its chain from one of the beams.

On the well-scrubbed walnut table two pewter plates were set, one on each side.

And now Philomene brought the kettle and set it on the table, on a round of pine wood made especially for it. She sat down and took her place without speaking.

Philomene began to eat her soup; it was the twenty-second of June, and, two thousand feet below, the Rhône went on flowing down in the plain, rubbing itself against the stones of its bed and stirring the air into light vibrations with a sound like dry leaves blowing.

All of a sudden Philomene stopped eating with the big pewter spoon halfway to her mouth. She looked at her daughter.

"What's the matter with you?"

"Nothing."

"Why aren't you eating, then?"

"I don't know," said Therese. "I'm not hungry."

Philomene shrugged her shoulders. "Oh, it's easy enough to see why. Because he isn't here. Look, my poor girl, you're not the only one these things happen to. I've been married too. . . . And when your poor father went up on the mountain, he left me all alone here for the summer, just like you. . . ."

Without realizing it, she still felt resentful about her daughter's marriage and her tone was hard.

"And then, after all, you picked him yourself, your husband, or didn't you? You ought to know what to expect, you were born here; you certainly

know that all the women are widows for two
months every year. . . ."

But Therese shook her head. "It isn't that."

"No? Well, what then?"

"I don't know . . ."

The twenty-second of June, around nine o'clock
in the evening, under the oil lamp with its little
yellow heart-shaped flame.

"You don't know?"

"Oh," she said, "I feel a little sick to my
stomach."

"Sick to your stomach?"

"Yes, and then I get dizzy sometimes."

"H'm," said Philomene. "Since when?"

"Just today."

"It's your month?"

"Yes," said Therese. That was all.

And now for the first time since her daughter's
marriage Philomene began to smile. She looked
at Therese.

"Oh," she said, "if that's it, that's a good kind
of sickness to have. One that you bow to politely
when it comes to find you. . . ."

Once again Therese felt the blood rising to her
face and making a layer of warmth just under her
skin. Then it subsided.

"Surely that's it!" Philomene was saying. "Oh,
that's a good kind of sickness, sure enough. You

mustn't be afraid. And you mustn't force yourself either. If you aren't hungry, don't eat. I'll
make you a cup of camomile tea and then you can
go to bed."

And she went on, "He doesn't know anything
about it, of course? Good! There'll be a fine surprise for him when he comes down."

She had gone to bed.

It was in their own house, which had been fixed
up especially for them. The big square bed was
made of larch wood and pegged to the wall. It rose
nearly to the ceiling on its high legs, and was as
wide as it was long.

I could sleep crosswise on it when he isn't here
with me.

But he will come down soon, he will come down
from the mountain, and then I'll say to him, "My
lord, come into the bed."

She kept thinking of him, because the bed was
too large for one. She would say, "You smell of
the mountain, of mud and smoke. Never mind, my
lord," she went on to herself, "come close to me
just the same, because I am cold and lonely."

Why should they have made the bed so wide, if
it wasn't for two people?

"I can sleep lengthwise in it, you see, and I can

sleep crosswise when you aren't here. But I'm tired of that; come quick close to me."

She would say, "Lie down there, but remember, you mustn't touch me. First of all I have to tell you something. It's a secret. Promise you won't tell anybody. Promise?"

I'll hold his hands still, if I have to. I'll say, "Don't touch me. My lord, O my gracious lord, what you are doing is forbidden."

And he: "A little kiss, just one?"

"Where?"

"On the eyelid."

"No," she would tell him. "Because I have something to tell you first. Put your head this way, looking up, and I'll lay mine flat on the pillow. Now your whiskers won't stick me, and I'll have my mouth right next to your ear. That's because of the secret. Antoine . . ."

She turned over again in the big bed, and the hours of the night began to pass. Perhaps she dozed.

There must have been a storm somewhere.

He was saying, "What is this secret? Money? A visit?"

And she: "Guess!"

It was still storming. The noise she heard in her dreams slid easily into reality. And now she opened her eyes, she could still hear it. It was a roll of thunder. It growled and rumbled above the mountains to the north. She could hear it coming, bouncing and rattling overhead like a heavily loaded cart of firewood, passing over and going on to fling itself against the southern range, which threw it back again.

It came back overhead, grumbling and crashing.

The shutters were banging, a ladder fell down outside, and the casement windows in the bedroom blew wide open.

As she crossed the room to shut them she felt cold in her nightgown. But at the window she saw that there were no flashes of lightning, although the thunder still rolled overhead like beating surf, interspersed with sharp crashes.

The night was beautifully clear. Bathed in a flood of moonlight, the trees were twisting strangely, flinging up their arms with all the leaves standing on end. Then they fell back into tranquillity, becoming round and still again under the soft and brilliant rain of moonlight dripping down from leaf to leaf.

What was going on?

She could hear people talking under the kitchen window, in the street, and she went quickly into the next room. She had nothing on under her nightgown, her feet were bare.

Little by little the thunder was dying away.

Finally there were only occasional distant sounds, like the snaps and crackles of the roof boards in freezing weather. Then they ceased, and everything was quiet overhead. But everywhere in the village doors and windows were opening. Heads were thrust out of the windows and people were standing before their doors in the street.

"What is it?" everybody asked. They looked at each other first, then up at the sky. The stars were in their same old places, one of them big and red, one green, and one little white one, shining peacefully in the patches of sky visible between the houses. There were the twinkling stars and the round ones, the stars that moved through the night and the ones that stayed still.

The people were talking in the street.

"It's not a storm."

She was afraid to show herself too much.

The men had put on their trousers hurriedly, the women wore skirts over their nightgowns. A voice was saying, "How do we know it isn't?"

She was afraid to show herself because her nightgown didn't fit and kept slipping off her shoulder.

"How can we tell? Some storms are split in two by the mountain. It could be good weather here and storming over where the Germans live. . . ."

Everybody looked toward the mountain, visible here and there between the houses, but it rose peacefully up against the stars, quiet and still all the way to the top.

"What are you thinking of? We'd see the flashes."

"Flashes of what?"

"Lightning."

"Or else they're blasting somewhere," somebody said.

"You're crazy! I think it's an earthquake. My bed shook right under me."

"Mine too."

"At our house," said one of the Carrupts, "it was a barrel I didn't chock up well enough. It rolled right over against the cellar door."

The men were black and white shapes in the moonlight, the women leaning out of the little windows made black silhouettes, which blocked nearly all of the light.

"But the noise?"

"Oh!" said someone. "The noise! Earthquakes always make a noise."

"And the wind?"

"They make a wind."

"You think so?"

"I know."

"Well, now what?"

"Well, now it's all over."

"What'll we do, go back to bed?"

Somebody asked, "What time is it?"

And a voice answered, "Half-past two."

It was now the twenty-third of June.

Therese still listened, but the doors were shutting one after the other, the windows were closing, and everything became still again on the earth as it had in the sky. The only sound in the quiet village was the babble of the fountain, which would go on uninterrupted now until the morning.

5

ONLY MAURICE NENDAZ guessed what had happened. He was a lame man who walked with a cane.

He had broken his left hip long ago, cutting wood in the forest, and it had set crookedly so that he had one leg shorter than the other.

As he walked he lurched first to one side and then to the other.

While the windows were shutting and doors closing as people went indoors, he moved forward a bit in the alley until he was half-hidden in the angle of a hay barn. Then he called softly, "Hey, Justin!"

A boy of fifteen or sixteen, now almost alone on the street, turned his head.

"Are you sleepy?" Nendaz asked. "No? Well, get a coat on and come with me."

"Where are you going?"

"You'll see."

Justin went up to get dressed; Nendaz was all ready to go, with his hat on and his stick in his hand.

"You didn't tell anybody?" he asked when the other came back. "Good! We might as well let them sleep in peace a little longer."

His stick knocked against the stones and his footsteps rang out unevenly in the quiet darkness as he came down more heavily on his bad leg than on the other.

As soon as you leave the village the path to Derborence begins to climb along the slope of the hill, which is just one rock ledge after another, with only a few spiny bushes and scrubby, red-trunked pines growing between them. In the daylight you can see the path perfectly, slanting up the hill as straight as if drawn by a ruler, to a cleft in the rocks far above. There it disappears abruptly. But at that hour of the night, with the moon just hidden behind a cloud, it was all the two men could do to distinguish the rough places in the path. Without a lantern, they had to go slowly and pick their way over the uneven surface. Round stones rolled under their feet, slabs of schist rocked as they stepped on them, and sharp edges of rock jabbed unexpectedly at their feet.

They climbed slowly, Nendaz in front because he had trouble with his leg. For three-quarters of an hour or thereabouts he said nothing. Justin could see him faintly up ahead, leaning to one side, straightening up, leaning to the other, his right hand gripping the head of his cane. He breathed heavily, for it was hard work. From time to time he stopped for a moment without turning around, and Justin stopped too, seeing before him only a formless blur of deeper shadow in the night, a shape without a head, for Nendaz kept leaning forward against the slope.

But now the darkness around them was slowly lightening, as if somebody had dropped a bit of white paint in a pail full of a darker color and was stirring it round and round. They were getting close to the end of the straight line which the path made on the slope—the end of the straight line where the path vanished from view. At that moment, the blackness began to turn to gray, and the gray, in turn, became more and more transparent. Little by little, everything around them regained its true color. The pines became green, their trunks reddish, the wild roses on the bushes were white and pink. It was light, it would soon be broad daylight and now they could see again. The rocks rose up in front of them, barring the path. But they could also see that there was a cleft in the rocks.

Maurice Nendaz stopped abruptly. He listened; he said to Justin, "You hear?"

He leaned over empty space and so did Justin, who had come up to him. They listened, and what they heard was nothing. A familiar voice had stopped speaking.

The harsh roar which had always sounded there, five hundred yards straight down at the bottom of the gorge, was silent. Or at least it was becoming silent, being already weak and intermittent, as if it was being slowly strangled. It spoke less and less loudly, less and less often.

The gorge was a narrow fissure, a saber cut through the mountain.

For uncounted years the water had sawed the rock from top to bottom, like the sawyers who stand above and below an oak log, dragging their saw steadily up and down.

And so through the ages the water had carved (how patiently, how minutely!) a narrow gorge with vertical sides nearly touching in places. The stream flowing at the bottom could not be seen, but always before that morning its voice could be heard in a kind of continual long sigh, floating up between the walls and becoming louder as it echoed from rock to rock.

But now the noise of the water could no longer

be heard. Nendaz listened. He said, "It's just what I thought."

"The Lizerne?" said Justin.

"Yes."

"Well, what about it? Is it stopped up?"

The other nodded his head and straightened up. As the daylight grew, the two men could see that the path did not end at the cleft in the mountain, but turned sharply beyond it, making a right angle to follow up the course of the gorge.

It stretched in front of them for quite a long way, nearly level between the high cliffs and the ravine. At one point it crossed a tumbled pile of rocks, then it disappeared from sight around a turning.

And Nendaz, nodding his head once more, started up again. He pushed on to this turning from which there was a wide view far off to the north. Then he pointed. Something was hanging there in the air, something which had just appeared above a wooded shoulder of the mountain, something yellowish and gleaming in the morning light like a flat pine board. It was already rising above the near-by ridges.

"You see?"

Justin stared and nodded.

"You know what it is?"

He shook his head.

"You think it's mist, maybe? Or smoke? Or that it's the fog lifting? Look again. Because smoke curls, doesn't it? And fog goes in streamers, like shavings when the carpenter planes a board. But you see, that goes straight up, it's smooth. Can't you guess. . . ?"

Justin had no time to say whether he had guessed or not, somebody was coming on the path. They could hear stones rolling around the corner before they could see anybody. Then he appeared. A boy around fourteen years old, a little younger than Justin. He was all brown and gray — long brown trousers and a dirty shirt. First he ran, then he walked a few steps, then he ran again. He came straight toward the two men as if he didn't see them. But they could see him, and they could see, too, that his head was hurt. Blood had trickled on his cheek and dried there, mingled with tears. He was crying as he ran. The tears stopped for a minute as they watched. Then a great sob gathered in his throat. It seemed to be pushing him ahead, for he began to run faster.

"You know him?"

"Yes," said Justin. "It's one of the Donneloyes from Premier. Dsozet, his name is. He must have come down from Zamperon."

Then Nendaz opened his arms wide to bar the path, but the other, with his eyes full of tears, did not even seem to see. He came right on without stopping, straight toward Nendaz. Justin in his surprise had not even time to move before Nendaz had to step aside to avoid being jostled over the precipice which opened beside the path.

The boy ran on, unseeing.

He was far down the path when, recovering himself, Nendaz cried to Justin, "Hurry up! Run after him! Catch him! You've got to get to the village before he does. Go to the mayor, do you hear? Tell him to come with two or three men. . . ."

Justin had already started running; Nendaz began to shout.

"Tell him that it's at Derborence! The noise last night . . . the wind . . . and that smoke just now. . . . The Devil's Tower . . ."

He kept on shouting.

"The Devil's Tower! Fell down on the valley. . . ."

It was an hour later when he saw the stretcher coming.

Sometimes they bring down wounded animals on a litter, from high on the mountain. A goat with a broken leg, for example, or with a horn torn off in a fight. They tie it down to the stretcher and cover it with an old canvas. One man grasps the handles in front, the other holds them behind.

You can meet them sometimes like that on the mountain paths, walking slowly and carefully, first the right foot forward, then the left, stepping in unison to keep the rhythm steady.

You see them coming a long way off, and wonder, "What are they carrying?" Then a puff of wind lifts the canvas, or the animal itself pushes it up with its 'head, and you feel relieved, because you can see what it is. You can see its beard, the little tuft of hair under its chin, its lustrous eyes, bright and astonished, and its little muzzle, half-opened to show the pink tongue, and from which comes a quavering uncertain bleat.

They were certainly carrying a stretcher that morning. It was covered with a canvas, as usual. But it was not a goat that lay there. It was something heavier, something longer—long enough so that the burden was too big for the litter and part of it hung down over the front. It showed the outline of two legs. At the other end was a red and white checked pillow slip stuffed with hay, for his head. For it was a man who was being carried that morning, and a heavy load he made.

There were four of them to carry him, and they relayed each other two by two. Biollaz and Loutre, and two others, also from Zamperon. The two men who carried the litter went in front, and the two others followed empty-handed.

They walked that way five or six minutes at a time, taking turns on the narrow rocky path. And it was a long path for them, they had four or five hours of it altogether. They had to come down the whole length of the ravine under a ribbon of sky hardly wider or less tortuous than the gorge; and they came down steadily, two by two, arms stiffened, shoulders dragged down, necks stretched forward, the vein showing there swollen as big as a thumb, carefully stepping in unison—five or six minutes at a time until the next stop.

Then all four stood around the litter. They spoke to the man there, they said, "Barthelemy!"

They shook their heads.

"He doesn't hear."

One of them pulled a clump of grass from beside the path. Leaning awkwardly over the wounded man he wiped away the foam which showed at the corners of his mouth and which had spread so that he seemed to have another beard on top of his own, a rose-colored beard full of bubbles.

The man let himself be cared for. He said nothing; he did not move. He looked up at the sky with a vacant, clouded gaze. His eyes were wide open but unseeing, as if their gaze were turned inward.

He had a rose-colored beard on top of his short black one; he had a big face that had once been brown, that had once been ruddy with warm blood and stirred into life by the outdoors, but was now greenish-gray like a stone which has been rolling in moss, a worn and polished stone. For his skin, dusty and lifeless elsewhere, had a taut gleam wherever the bones held it up. And all of a sudden Barthelemy's breathing became shorter and faster, pushing out a new layer of foam over his beard. His chest had been crushed, and they were hurrying down to the village to try and save him.

The men who had put him down on the path called to him, shaking their heads as they stood under the narrow strip of sky in the ravine which even on the sunniest day was always shadowy and somber.

"Barthelemy," they said, "do you want a drink?"

One of them had a horn drinking-cup in his pocket, which he filled from the trickle of water beside the path. Then he leaned over, but the water only ran away uselessly on Barthelemy's chin, the water spread out around his mouth, which understood no longer, which refused everything, which said No.

The men bent to the stretcher again and started

down the path. Then they saw Nendaz coming to meet them.

He had gone on walking up the gorge with his bad leg and his cane, and had covered slowly part of the distance while they were coming down the rest.

The two men who carried nothing came ahead of the stretcher to meet him.

"Was it the mountain?" Nendaz asked.

The two men nodded.

"I knew that was it. Last night . . . And now," he said, pointing to the stretcher, "is that all there is left?"

The two men nodded.

"Of all of them who were up there?"

This time they spoke, "Yes."

"And at Zamperon?"

"There's one man with his arm broken. He'll be along presently, he was getting bandaged up."

Nendaz took off his hat and crossed himself. The two men did the same.

Then they asked: "Do they know about it yet down there?"

"No, they thought it was a storm."

"So they don't know."

"They probably do by now, though," said Nendaz. "A boy from your place went by a while ago, so I sent Justin down to tell them."

The men with the stretcher were approaching.

"Who is it?" Nendaz asked.

"Barthelemy."

"Ah," said Nendaz, "Barthelemy . . ."

He held his hat in his hand; he moved forward.

"Barthelemy, Barthelemy, it's me! Maurice Nendaz. Can you hear me? Barthelemy . . ."

6

PHILOMENE was awake early that morning. She opened her eyes with the feeling that something pleasant had happened to her the evening before. Then as she looked at the faint ash-gray light filtering through the partly opened shutters, she remembered. Yes, it was something pleasant. The idea of being a grandmother was a cheerful one. When a child comes, everything is comfortably settled.

Everything was settled or being planned out little by little in her head as she got dressed. She was thinking to herself, "Well, no use crying about spilt milk. They're married and there's nothing more to be done about it. Anyway, it looks as if it would be all right now." A child coming meant that things would go well. She would be needed, and for an old woman that would be like coming back into life, she thought to herself, feeling warm and contented already, while on the other side of the window the light grew slowly brighter.

She went on arranging things, and now she was saying to herself, as she thought of Therese, "I should never have let her go off to sleep alone last night. What could I have been thinking of? I should have kept her here. Everybody feels a bit nervous at the beginning."

But then she thought, "Oh well, I'll make her some soup now and take it over under a cloth to keep it warm, so she can eat before she gets up. It'll do her good to stay in bed a little."

Outside, a barn door opened. Somebody was going to milk his goat. There were hardly any cows left in the village, and not many more men. Vigorous, healthy men, that is; it was a village of goats, children, old people and women. On the barn door the rusty bolt made a great screech like the noise the pig makes when it is being slaughtered and the knife plunges into the big vein in its neck. Somebody coughed. The village fountain was a tree trunk, sawed down the middle and hollowed out. It was old Jean Carrupt who was coughing. The fountain was so mossy that from a distance you could hardly distinguish it from the grassy slope behind it, and instead of a pipe it had only a wooden trough, so leaky that half the water was lost before it got to the pool.

Old Jean Carrupt was always up early, and he was always thirsty. They were nearly all Carrupts in the village; the only way to distinguish one from another was to use their given names or nicknames.

Jean Carrupt had been to the fountain for a drink; he came away slowly, dragging his feet.

Philomene had lit the fire and hung the kettle on the hook. People were beginning to move about under the windows in the lovely rose-colored light of dawn, which had appeared first in the eastern sky, then flowed softly down over the village.

Old Jean's back was all rosy, in the ancient coat which he had worn for more than twenty years.

His back was turned as he looked up at the slope which rises up behind the village.

Smoke curled from the chimneys into the slowly brightening sky.

Suddenly old Jean mumbled something to himself.

"What did you say, Uncle Jean?" asked one of the women at the fountain.

He grumbled something again.

"Well, I declare, that's right! Marie! Can you see? Up there, on the path."

"Who is it?"

"I don't know."

"What are they doing?"

71

"Oh, when they're young, they're bound to play. . . ."

And indeed, as the two boys came running down the path, it looked just like a game of tag. Dzoset was in front, Justin behind. When the one behind ran faster, so did the one in front, as if to avoid being caught. For the game is to tag each other, and the one who succeeds wins.

The women were watching.

"Where are they going?"

"Why are they running so hard?"

Now they could see that the first boy's lead was diminishing little by little, in spite of his efforts, and now the other forced his pace, he came abreast. And everybody was surprised, for he didn't tag the leader or catch hold of him, as they had expected. He simply passed him by without saying a word, without even looking at him.

"It's Justin. Wherever is he coming from like that? He was here last night, wasn't he?"

"Of course he was. I saw him myself."

So it is that misfortune approaches, on two legs, or twice two legs, without anybody recognizing it; that bad news comes, and comes running, but nobody guesses what it is. Now that he was close the women were calling to Justin.

"Hey, Justin!"

He didn't answer. He left the path and cut

72

through the back gardens on the run as if to avoid being questioned as he went by. As for young Dsozet, he had turned off into the path to Premier without coming into the village at all, and was already out of sight.

Philomene had come out on her doorstep when she heard the women's voices. They were scattering between the houses trying to see Justin and find out who he was after, for it was easy to guess that he was looking for somebody. Finally he stopped at the mayor's house, right at the other end of the village. It stood beside the building where Rebord served out drinks, in his second-story room at the end of a wooden staircase as steep as a ladder.

Justin went into the mayor's house, he came out with the mayor, and it was then that misfortune reached the village. For as Justin appeared again he lifted his arm and pointed toward the north. First he gestured with both arms, then using only one he pointed again toward the mountains. The mayor nodded. The mayor looked around him, took a step forward, then stopped as if he could do no more. He was a little old man with a white mustache; Crettenard was his name. He brought his hand up falteringly to his mustache, smoothed it, then suddenly shrugged his shoulders. For a moment they stayed that way, right up to his ears. A great silence fell over the village, in which they could hear a cock crowing derisively, then suddenly Rebord came running down his staircase.

His hurrying feet sounded like a roll of drums. A man's voice said, "It can't be true."

A woman cried out, "Ah! . . . Ah! . . . Ah! . . ."

A long cry, three times repeated, each time higher, until it broke off like a dry reed in the wind.

All at once the village was full of noise and motion. Everybody was running toward the mayor and Justin.

"It's the mountain?"

"Yes."

"And then what? To fall on Derborence! It isn't possible! What do you think you're talking about?"

"Don't you remember the noise last night?"

Some of them were weeping, women called out shrilly, children were crying. They pushed and jostled in the alley as they pressed forward; it was disaster that had been on the way, and now at last they understood that it had come. Four or five men stood around the mayor.

Some of the women laughed and said, "Nonsense! Nonsense! It's just a pack of lies."

"I don't know," the mayor kept saying. "I don't know, I tell you. Let me alone, I'll have to go and see. . . ."

Philomene had come forward too; she slipped through the crowding women, opening up a path between the gesticulating arms and the moving heads.

"Well?" she said, "well, Mr. Mayor?"

He came forward.

"I don't know anything. Ask Justin."

"Well, you then," she asked Justin, "what about Seraphin? . . ."

"I don't know."

"And Antoine?"

"I don't know."

She had started running as fast as she could toward her daughter's house. It stood a little apart from the center of the village, and still looked quiet and asleep. The outside door was unlocked and Philomene stepped into the kitchen.

She knocked on the bedroom door.

"Is that you, Mother?"

"Yes."   . . . .

She went in and said immediately, "You've got the windows open, you'll catch cold."

And she went quickly to shut them.

"You have to be careful now, you know, in your condition. Did you sleep well? Oh, it was I who waked you up? Well, never mind. I felt a little uneasy about you. That's why I came over."

The closed windows with their heavy bottle-glass panes shut out nearly all sounds from outside.

Philomene was fussing with the little curtains disturbed by the wind in the night. It seemed to be taking her a long time to rearrange them.

"You'd better stay in bed this morning," she said. "It's more sensible. I'll bring your soup over. . . ."

Her back was still turned. She could hear Therese saying: "Oh, no. I'm going to get up."

"You're feeling better then?"

"Oh, yes," said Therese. "As a matter of fact, I feel fine today."

Suddenly they heard a cry, piercing through the walls and the thick glass. Footsteps pounded by the front of the house.

"What's that?"

"Oh, nothing," said Philomene.

"But Mother, what's the matter with you?"

For she couldn't put it off for ever. In the end she had to turn around, showing her white face and her hands clutched together at her waist to keep them from trembling.

And in spite of the half darkness Therese was staring at her, for nobody can keep the truth from coming out.

"Nothing's the matter."

"That's funny," Therese said.

Somebody was knocking at the front door. Who could it be?

Therese could hear her mother talking in the kitchen, and then another woman's voice answering in a low tone. Outside in the street the noise was growing louder as it approached the house.

"What's happening?" Therese asked again.

The two women came in. The other was her mother's sister, Catherine.

"Oh," said Catherine, "don't pay any attention. It's Barthelemy's wife, she's all upset . . . her baby is sick. . . ."

The two of them stood still by the door, shaken and trying to appear calm, rooted to the spot although they wanted to come forward, knowing that something had to be said, but finding nothing to say. Philomene's hands were trembling more and more on her striped apron.

"Just a minute," said Therese. "I'm going to get up."

"No," said Catherine. "No, you'd much better stay in bed."

But just then the church bell sounded. It began to toll: a stroke, then a stroke, then another stroke.

Barthelemy had just died. The men who were

carrying him could tell that he was dead because his mouth stayed open in his beard.

They were almost in the village. They set the stretcher down on the path. Then the four of them, with Nendaz, stood around it bareheaded, and they were joined by the people who had come to meet them (that was why the noise had gone by Therese's house): the mayor, Justin, Rebord, men, women and children.

The women knelt down, one by one, while somebody went running off toward the chapel.

A stroke. The bell tolled again.

"Who's dead?" Therese asked.

"Oh," said Catherine (and it was hard for her to find the right words), "it must be the baby. Yes, of course, it must be. His poor mother!"

"He wasn't sick yesterday."

"Yes, it's Barthelemy's baby . . . his mother said he had croup . . . it came on in the night."

A stroke.

"She was running from house to house like a madwoman. As if we others could do anything. . . ."

A stroke. Up on the path the women were rising to their feet. The men took up their load again, one at each end of the stretcher. They had pulled the canvas over the dead man's face.

And yet a great peace reigned on the mountain-

tops which soared into the sky above them. From
the place which the dead man was leaving it was
still possible to see far over the roofs of the village to the great hollow where the valley dropped
away. That morning it was brimming with a soft
morning mist on which two broad bands of sun
and shadow lay side by side, invisibly sewn together like the stripes on a flag. Above it the
mountains grew brighter and still more bright
until at last they shone out tranquilly, rank on
rank of peaks, of towers, of battlements, floating
in gold and silver against the blue, and seeming to
move a little, as the flames of church candles move
when somebody passes by.

—All is tranquillity on the mountain tops, all
is rest — for me there will be no more rest.—

The dead man left his place. They made him
leave his place, he didn't say no, he let himself
be taken. He went down the path a little further.
And the others came after him. They were crying
more softly now, they didn't even dare talk to
each other, they had silenced their tears which
fell without a sound.

—And rest. But for me, there will be no more
rest, no, never again in this life.—

For although her mother and her aunt tried to
hold her back, they were not strong enough.
Therese ran across the room, she stood by the

window. And then she saw. First of all came Barthelemy on his stretcher, a man at his head, another at his feet, and he himself lying still. They stood upright, he was lying down; they walked forward, he was motionless and acquiescent under his canvas. First there were his feet hanging over the edge of the stretcher, then the raised place in the canvas where his head lay on the pillow. Tranquillity, rest. First he came, and after him came all the others.

Old Carrupt went to meet them. He didn't understand very well what was happening and from time to time he gave a little grumble as he talked to himself.

Therese stood by the window.

"Oh," she said, "that's a fine thing! There's been an accident and you try to hide it from me!"

Her mother and her aunt tried to pull her away: Barthelemy's wife was coming with her six children.

The bell went on tolling. A stroke, then a stroke, then another stroke.

A stroke. Barthelemy's wife held the smallest child in her arms and gave a hand to another who was just learning to walk, while two others sheltered behind her skirts. She had six children.

There was Nendaz with his cane — Therese recognized him.

Nendaz walked down the street.

He was one among all the others who passed and who seemed only a little higher than the ground, as high as the line of little low windows in the wooden walls — she saw their full or pointed beards, their hair, tangled or cut short, or else the women's long hair, wound into a knot behind; brown, black, even blond. . . .

"That's a fine thing!"

Then to Nendaz: "Hurry up and tell me. What happened?"

For now Barthelemy was under the window. She could look down and see him passing under the window, lying flat, his face covered. She could see that he lay motionless; and his wife began to sob again, letting her tears run down her face into her mouth. They made dark spots on her gray blouse.

Some of the women lifted their arms in the air or pressed their hands on each side of their heads. But the men walked with their heads bowed: the mayor, Justin, Rebord, Nendaz, the others — not very many of them, alas, because of all the dead up yonder . . . Not many men, and no more for years to come, it was a little village, a little village of goats, women, children and old men. And all this while Nendaz moved forward with the others until he was below Therese, and she spoke to him.

"What happened?"

She was still speaking only about Barthelemy.

"I think he must be dead. Is it true, Maurice Nendaz?"

Nendaz went by with his cane.

"Why doesn't he answer me? Good Lord, it's funny. What's the matter with everybody? Justin!"

Justin didn't seem to hear; he walked on too and was already past the window.

A woman looked up at Therese.

"You don't know? You don't know yet . . . ? Oh God . . ."

She broke off in the middle of her sentence. It was as if she had already forgotten Therese.

"Don't stay there at the window, you'll catch cold," begged Philomene. "We'll explain . . ."

"Explain what?"

But the explanation didn't wait. One of the women looked up. "The mountain has fallen."

"What mountain?"

"The Devil's Tower."

"Fallen? Fallen where?"

"On Derborence."

Then Therese said, "And the men . . . ?"

But suddenly she began to laugh.

"The mountain!"

She laughed again.

"It doesn't just fall down like that, a mountain!"

Then, all of a sudden:

"And Antoine, where is he?"

She cried out:

"Oh, Antoine, my husband! Antoine, my own darling!"

7

THEY CALCULATED later that more than a hundred and fifty million cubic feet had fallen in the avalanche. A hundred and fifty million cubic feet of rock—that's going to make a noise when it hits bottom. It had made a great noise, one that had been heard from one end to the other of the valley, although this was two leagues wide and nearly fifteen long. At first, though, people did not know what the noise meant.

Now they were going to find out. The news had begun to travel, and travel fast, in spite of the fact that in those days there were no telegraph lines, no telephones, and no cars. It was quickly told. All people needed to say was, "The mountain has fallen."

The news had arrived almost as quickly at Premier as at Aire, because of young Dsozet. He stood beside the fountain while the blood was being washed from his face, and the news came from his mouth and ran from house to house.

Always, in that country, there are the mountains above you, moving when you move, brilliantly white in the blue sky which seems to curve and lower itself to meet you, like the roof of a cave. Under this sky the news travelled onward.

First it followed the road, then it left the road and ran straight downhill, jumping the hedges.

A man working in the fields lifted his head.

"What's going on?"

"The mountain."

"What mountain?"

The little lizards sunning themselves on the stones ran into their holes.

"Derborence . . ."

The news passed on and travelled further, heading always toward the great valley where the ground breaks away sharply in two tones of color between the pines. It tumbled down the steep slopes and through the vineyards to where the Rhône hits you in the face suddenly with its white fire.

There stood a little town where around eleven o'clock a doctor was getting on his horse, his instrument case tied on behind the saddle.

Before noon the news had arrived at the county seat, and there was a great hubbub of voices in the cafés.

People were drinking the muscatel of that region.

"Derborence!"

A wine so golden it is almost brown, a wine all warm on the palate, with an aftertaste of new grapes and a perfume which rises up the back of your nose as you drink.

"It seems there's not a man left!" people said.

"And the cows?"

"Not a one!"

They came out on the doorsteps of the houses to look up, but the town was so far away from the mountains that they could see nothing. Nothing at all. Or at the most, way off to the west behind the rocks, a tiny grayish cloud, as transparent as muslin, lay flat against the sky.

Until six o'clock in the evening hardly anybody had gotten up as far as the mountain. Only the people of Zamperon were there. And not many of those, for only five or six — one of them a woman — had stayed in the village. They put the cows to pasture in the fields close by, to save watching them, and went immediately to work, one holding a hammer, another a pick, as they tried to free a jammed door or put slates back on the roofs.

While they were working two men from Anzeindaz showed up. They had made a long detour around the cliffs to avoid the landslide.

They came. They said nothing at first. They came and said nothing. They looked at the people from Zamperon who said nothing either. Then they nodded their heads slowly.

And they said, "Well?"

The people from Zamperon said, "Yes," and nodded their heads.

"Ah," said the others, "it's a great misfortune! Were there any who were able to save themselves?"

"One."

"One?"

"Only one. And in what a state! They've just taken him down."

It was a little hard for them to understand each other because they didn't speak the same dialect; still, the men from Anzeindaz began again.

"We came down to see if you needed any help. If you do, we could send down a crew of men."

But the others shook their heads.

"Thanks, thank you very much, but we can manage all right. Everything we need at least. As for them . . ."

They pointed up the hollow to Derborence, then they let their hands fall to their sides.

"They don't need anybody any more."

They all sat down together for a minute, on a wall in the sun, and began to drink brandy from the flask that the men from Anzeindaz had brought along in a bag, with some bandages. While they were there the Germans from Sanetsch came down for the news too. For a long time before they arrived you could see them clambering down the narrow chimneys of rock in the Woodcutter's Passage, one above the other, as if they were on a rope ladder. First they were visible from below, then hidden, then seen again, as the white clouds which clung to the rock walls parted or closed in on them.

Finally they came. Since they spoke only German, they tried to make themselves understood by gestures. So there were men from three cantons come together for a moment to drink brandy together; the men from Anzeindaz came from the west, those of Sanetsch from the northeast.

They passed the cup back and forth as they sat side by side, looking across the stream in front of them, toward the shoulder of the mountain where the young pines had been flattened out the night before. They could see that the trees were all lying in the same direction — away from the blast of wind — and that some of them were broken off at ground level, others halfway up, as if it were a field of wheat that had been mowed in a dry season with too dull a scythe.

They talked each in his own language.

Passing the cup back and forth, they sat in the sun. Below them the big rocks scattered in the bed of the stream were already drying out and the little oval pools between them, gleaming like eyeglasses in the sun, were full of silence. The great voice of the water was silent, though the men, astonished by the strange new stillness, still kept straining their ears instinctively to hear its long-accustomed roar. And as they became still in their turn, by obeying the silence, they added to it.

One after another they stopped speaking. Then the men from Anzeindaz and those from Sanetsch started back up the mountain. Zamperon was quiet again.

But Aire was full of people. Many had come there almost at once from Premier, which had a big population and was the parish center where the priest lived.

The doctor arrived around noon, his horse lathered and white with foam.

The man with a broken arm was there too: a young man around twenty years old, called Placide Fellay. He was sitting in a kitchen while the doctor, surrounded by splints and bandages, reduced his fracture.

Two men held him by the shoulders and legs.

As for the dead man, all that was needed there was to verify that he was really dead — this twenty-third of June. More people kept on arriving. The doctor bent over the bed where Barthelemy lay and listened to his heart. There was nothing to listen for any more. They had tied a cloth around Barthelemy's head to keep his mouth closed.

Someone brought a mirror, first rubbing it to a bright polish on his knee, and the doctor held it before Barthelemy's mouth. The mirror remained as brilliant as before.

The doctor straightened up. He shook his head.

"Ahhhhhhhh!"

A long wail of sorrow, three times repeated, and heard clear out in the street. The people walking by stopped for a minute.

"It's Barthelemy's wife."

The doctor was getting ready to leave for Derborence, with two or three men and a mule loaded with provisions. The coroner had just arrived.

They questioned Biollaz, but he only said, "You'll see, all right. . . ."

Biollaz and Loutre were together, and Biollaz was saying, "Stones, enormous stones, bigger than . . ."

He pointed to the houses along the street.

90

"Two or three times bigger than our houses. They've blocked up the stream. The Lizerne. They're all on top of the pasture. What do you think would be left after that?"

"Barthelemy got out, didn't he?" they said.

"Oh, him!" said Biollaz. "The point there was that his cabin was off to one side, and a little above the others. Besides, look at him, even he didn't miss it, did he? He would have been better off to have been killed right away, the way it turned out."

"How many does that make, then?" they asked.

He answered, "That makes nineteen. Fifteen from Aire, and four men from Premier."

"And how many cows?"

"Lord!" he said, "at least a hundred and fifty. And then the goats too. . . ."

But it was time to start. The mule was all loaded and the men going on the expedition left without waiting any longer.

Sorrow in the house, and in the next. Here, and here again, and there, and again further on. Over there, somebody was laughing. People said it was the wife of the dead man who had lost her wits.

Strangers kept walking through the village. They stopped, they looked, they shook their heads.

Old Jean Carrupt, who didn't understand very

well what was going on, went on wandering around, grumbling to himself from time to time.

In one house after another, misfortune. Here, and here, and over there, while the world stopped and looked on. From the houses came voices, sobs, wails, then nothing. You could hear laughter and weeping at the same time.

The landslide at Derborence, on the twenty-third of June—only ten days after the men had gone up on the mountain.

"If only they had waited a little!" people said.

"How could they? It was the time to go. They just went up as they always had."

"I don't believe a word of it!"

It was Therese. They had got her back to bed, and her mother and her aunt were staying with her. Every few minutes somebody knocked on the door.

"Oh," said Catherine to everybody, "please don't come in, don't come in. It would be better to let her stay quiet."

The people passing by the house stopped to look.

"There too. Yes, there were two from there. Her husband and her mother's brother."

"Antoine Pont."

"And Seraphin Carrupt."

So the dead were named over and one by one

were numbered. At the top of the stair, when the door was opened, glowed the reflection of the big fire burning on the kitchen hearth.

It seemed that she was expecting a child.

Water was heating in the kettle hung over the fire and in her bed Therese was saying, "Look, how can a mountain just fall down, like that? You make me laugh. . . ."

She was working herself up, tossing and turning, and as she seemed feverish, they kept putting cold compresses on her forehead.

"If mountains fall down like that for no reason, what's going to happen to the rest of us? We've got plenty of mountains around here too. . . ."

She turned over impatiently again.

"Take these compresses off!"

Swallowing her tears, Philomene begged, "Oh, Therese, please! Please!"

"Leave me alone, can't you? I'm all right. . . ."

"It's not just you. There's someone else to think of now."

"Who else?"

She lay quiet, thinking. Suddenly she asked, "What's all that noise?"

"People."

"What people?"

"People who've come to hear the news."

"It's true then," she said. "It must be true if

there are people here. The mountain . . . Oh!"
she asked her mother, "you, do you really think
he's dead?"

"Nobody knows yet. We have to wait. We don't
know anything. They've only just left."

"Who?"

"The doctor and the coroner."

"So," she said, "we have to wait? How long?"

"Till tomorrow or the day after. We promise
we'll tell you everything."

"Oh," she said, "it doesn't matter."

She turned over again.

"What are they making such a fuss about?"
she asked.

Suddenly she sat up in bed.

"Couldn't I go with them? Couldn't I?"

Her mother and her aunt ran to her, trying to
make her lie down again.

"My poor girl, what good do you think you
could do up there? Look, all there is to do is wait.
You'll have to wait just like us. For what do you
think we could possibly do, I'm just asking you,
what could we do, my poor child?"

And she went on, through the tears running
down her cheeks, "And then, you ought to think
of him."

"Who?"

"The baby. Your baby that's coming."

"All right!"

She let them lay her down in bed and rested quietly again on the pillow. She crossed her hands on the sheet.

The mountains would soon be glowing with evening color again.

—The mountains are falling on our heads. The mountains are beautiful, but they're wicked too.—

"And if I have a child?" she asked. "If I have Antoine's child? I know well enough Antoine will never come back. But then the baby, he'll be half an orphan, he will have lost his father even before he is born. Oh!" she said, "just the same, it would have made Antoine happy! I would have whispered the secret into his ear . . . Well, now I will tell him nothing. He will never know about it, never. It's funny."

And suddenly she cried out, "No! I don't want it! I don't want it! A child with no father, it isn't a child at all! Get rid of it for me, I don't want it!"

SECOND PART

1

Two months, or nearly two months, had passed.

People had come to the mountain. They clambered over the great pile of rock. They had all the time they needed to hunt from one end to the other through the tumbled stones of its surface. They found nothing. Nothing anywhere, not a single person, living or dead. Cabins, animals and men had disappeared completely under the stones.

Then came the Federal engineers, taking their turn after the doctor, the coroner, and the throngs of curious spectators. They were there to estimate the volume of the landslide: a hundred and fifty million cubic feet.

They, too, had all the time they needed while they took their measurements. They unrolled their long tapes, with the little black division marks, laying them flat against the rocks, first across the valley, then down its length. Then one of the men climbed to the top of what seemed to

be the highest boulder in the mass, trying to estimate its depth.

They calculated the size of the avalanche so that
the necessary changes could be made in the maps;
so that what was indicated on the records as pastures and fertile fields could be replaced by the
notation: "waste land."

The survey took a long time, but they had all
the time in the world to complete it. No one in-
terfered with them as they worked. The people
who came out of curiosity grew fewer and fewer
as the days went by, and the world of nature was
peaceful and acquiescent, having returned to rest,
to immobility, to indifference. Finally, last of all,
came scientists from the city, who climbed up as
far as the glacier and went carefully all over it,
looking for any fresh crevasses that might spell a
new danger, either imminent or in the distant fu-
ture. But everything seemed to be securely in its
proper place. The beautiful white sheet of snow
was untorn and swept smoothly from edge to edge
of the icefield which lay almost flat behind the
crest.

Little by little the clouds of dust had risen
above the surrounding walls, and then blown
away. The valley of Derborence was now completely visible. The air which had been opaque
and swirling with dust was now clear and trans-

parent, and the sightseers who came as far as the valley had only to tip their heads back to see, high up at the extreme frontier between earth and sky, the place where the landslide had broken off. Before the catastrophe the rock had jutted out at this point and hung over empty space, surmounted with a heavy load of bristling ice pinnacles. Now what had once stood out in relief against the sky was hollow, what had been convex was concave. The bulge of the rock had been replaced with a vast and steeply inclined gully. Its contents had been emptied, all at once, on the pasture, which then had ceased to be a pasture, on those who lived there, who lived there no longer, on everything alive, which had been instantly deprived of life. The immobility and the stillness of death reigned over the valley. There was only one moving object: high up in the gully a muddy mass, a kind of sluggish river of sand and earth and water, still oozed downhill. Confined and channelled by its high borders, it moved gradually down until it spread itself noiselessly on the cone of debris below. It was silent, slowly advancing; its flow so imperceptible that you had to look carefully a long time to make sure it was moving at all.

A collection had been taken up through the countryside, and this did a little to help out those families who had lost their livestock. In addition they had been allotted new pasturage rights on land owned elsewhere by the community, to replace those they had lost at Derborence.

There was not much else to do, a small correction to make on the map, an annotation to write into the survey book. It might perhaps be necessary to redraw the map eventually, for there the valley was still outlined in green.

And green signifies grass, and grass means life.

Nothing up there any more but old Plon with his flock of sheep, and the flock wandered through the ravines like a cloud shadow.

It had to keep moving all the time. Nothing grew in those solitudes but a little thin grass in the cracks between the stones, as if between the cobbles in a paved court: the sheep had to hunt for it blade by blade. The flock moved forward, grazing as it went. It drifted over the mountain like a shadow, and as it moved its shape changed continuously; first round, then pointed, then triangular and again like a square. Now on the slopes, now down in a hollow, it looked exactly like the shadow of a cloud whose outline shifts and changes as it sails across the sky. The flock moved ahead, its shape like a crescent as it passed

over a little hill, then bulging forward in the other
direction as it went down into a hollow. The hundreds of little hooves pattered like rain, and the
teeth snatching at the grass made a noise like little
waves continually striking on a pebbled beach.

Near-by, old Plon was always standing, like a
wintry old fir tree firmly rooted in the ground.

Rooted there, upright in his cape and old rag-
ged hat, he nodded his white beard above the cape.

"D . . . D . . E . ."

He laughed to himself.

"Nobody left. . . nobody left? Oh, you think
so, do you?"

And he went on, "The engineers have all gone
home, and a good thing too . . . But that doesn't
prove it. Just because they've left . . ."

He began again.

"D . . E . . . D . . E . . V . . I . ."

Just then a stone broke loose from the river of
mud and struck the rocks below with a sound like
a laugh.

"I hear you," he said. "You understand me all
right, don't you?"

The whole great wall of rock began to laugh as
the echoes spread to left and right and blended
into one vast murmuring chuckle. All the mountain burst out laughing, and he answered:

"Yes, you understand. I don't need to go on, do I? You know your own name."

Little by little the mountain quieted down. From rock to rock the laughter died into silence, while old Plon stood and waited.

"Yes, you know what's going on all right," he said to the mountain. "I know, and you know too. You make things happen just because you don't care what you do. But the one behind it all, you know him, don't you? You know him well. D . . E . . V . . I . . . You can hear them, just as I do at night, all the poor fellows that he keeps imprisoned here. While I'm in my little stone hut at night, and you're up there high against the sky. . . . That's what they say, isn't it? That the dead walk at night, lamenting and wailing because they have no rest? With shapes like bodies, but nothing inside. . . . Empty shells, but they make a noise at night, and people can see them, can't they?"

The mountain began to laugh again.

Then, suddenly, there was this head. But the rocks stood so thickly around the spot where it emerged that nobody could see it.

2

HE GOT his head out.

It was nearly two months after the landslide.
He crawled out of a hole. First his head squeezed
between two stones — out into daylight. Nobody
saw him.

Only the eagle could have seen him, the mountain eagle, soaring overhead on his strong wings
and turning on the earth below that piercing
scrutiny which can distinguish instantly moving
objects from still ones, living from lifeless matter. The eagle is above everything, and no matter
how high he soars, his little gray eyes notice the
slightest change in the pattern of the world below. They see the hare gambolling on the slope,
the baby marmot just coming out of his hole.

As for the head, nobody saw it. It was too little,
too lost in the great waste of stone.

Only the eagle might have noticed it, because
the head moved and the stones around it did not

move. The eagle circles slowly on his great wings, tipping them only enough to catch the wind, like the sails of a ship. He veers and turns, sailing far off on his great circle of air, sweeping back again, and dominating from his great height that immense hollow below where the boulders seem no bigger than scattered gravel.

It was down there that something was moving. In the last hour or two the sun had risen above the mountains. Now it shone full on the hollow, and something moved and moved again in a little patch of shadow there like a drop of ink on a gray blotter.

You could have seen him from high up in the air, but only from there, when he first got his head out. At first his head was the only thing to show above the rocks.

You would have to have been high enough to say to the eagle, "Lower yourself a little, come down and look! Leave the heights and drop closer."

But then, pausing in his descent, he would have hesitated, for man is not his prey, and he is afraid of man.

Though it was only a poor sort of a man who came out from under the ground, a miserable remnant of a man, appearing in a crack between the haphazard tumble of rocks; come out of the sha-

dow, out of unimaginable depths, out of the night;
and now struggling toward the day.

He was lighter than the shadow which still surrounded him; his skin was pale and his shoulders
gleamed whitely under his rags. He got his head
out, he lifted his head.

From where he was he could see nothing.

When he looked up there was nothing to see
but the blue of the sky. The sky was smooth and
flat, cut out in a circle and stretched tightly overhead like the paper cover on a jam pot.

Inside his crack, a fault in the rock which wid-
ened as it came to the surface, he raised himself
on his hands and knees. He was still partly hidden, then he moved forward and his head came to
the edge of the shadow.

The sun struck his head.

He stopped again.

His hair was long and fell raggedly down the
nape of his neck.

Finally he flung his hands away from his eyes.
His hands clung to each side of his head above
his ears, as limp as wet rags.

His eyelids fluttered. He shut his eyes, opened
them, shut them again.

There he was, with his head in the sun, and he
was no longer accustomed to it. He had to get used

to the sun again—the sunlight was beautiful, but it hurt; it felt good, but it burned too.

He felt like a small child who has been made to drink a wine tonic. The blood rang in his ears, and he couldn't tell if the humming was inside or outside him, for he had lost the faculty of hearing and the power of sight, lost the happy gift of telling the colors, lost his taste, his smell, and the ability to recognize shapes and distinguish distances.

He shut his eyes, he opened them. Then he put his fingers in his ears and shook his head like a dog coming out of the water. And little by little the sweetness of life began to steal over him, murmuring to him with its sun, its colors, and all its good things, and wrapping him in comfort like a warm suit of clothes all over his body.

He breathed deeply as if he were drinking.

The air came into his body, it had a taste and a perfume, it flowed softly through his lungs and his belly, bringing strength back with it. After a little he began to climb again. He clambered up between two big boulders that stood high above the tumbled stones until he reached the top of one of them and could see out widely over the valley.

There he stretched out on a slab of rock.

Now his body was all bathed in sunlight, he was

surrounded by it, completely under the dominion of the sun, and now at last he had room enough. There was even more room than he needed.

He stretched his legs out comfortably and yawned. He raised his arms above his head and swept them down in a wide arc to his sides. They didn't touch anything, they touched nothing but the air, which was soft and elastic, giving way at a touch and then flowing gently back again.

It felt good. "It feels good," he said aloud and yawned again. He scratched his head, his neck, his back and legs. He was out of the shadow now, he was all visible. He was a grayish-white color like a turnip, and his toes stuck out of the broken ends of his shoes. One trouser leg was torn off at the knee, the other split up at the side. He lay sprawled out at his ease. Then he yawned again and leaned on his other elbow. He had on what was left of a coat, torn right up to his shoulders in back and wide open in front, showing his hollow chest. His chin was covered with a stubby tough beard.

He was the same color all over, from head to foot, clothes and all, a color which grew lighter and lighter as the sunlight touched it. Everything —leather, cloth, canvas, his own skin and hair— was the same dirty gray now turning to white.

After a while he took an old crust of black

bread from his pocket and holding it to his mouth
with both hands he began to munch loudly.

Flies and more flies came to circle around him,
and butterflies too, little white butterflies, and
others colored a delicate gray and blue. They rose
and fell, floating limply on the air like bits of
torn tissue paper, while he ate gluttonously, lick-
ing in his saliva, the center of a little black cloud
of circling insects.

While he ate he looked around him. He could
see again. Now everything was no longer on a single plane. Some things were in front, others behind, and objects again had greater or lesser
distances between them. Space organized itself
around him in perspective, in height and depth.
The sun helped him. The sun wanted to keep him
from seeing, but it couldn't do it. Man makes the
sun help him—if you don't want to help me see,
I'll make you just the same, and that thing over
there is a pebble, see, it's a pebble! He saw the
shattered rocks all around him. Where they had
split, the surfaces were clean and unweathered,
gleaming in the sun; some of them were blue with
white veins, some as purple as a periwinkle, or
chestnut brown, and others were like clover blos-
soms or blackened as if by fire. There were rocks
everywhere, as many rocks as a man could want
for the rest of his life, or have time to look at, and

as they stretched far off in their piled-up masses
or jumbled heaps it was impossible for him to believe in what he saw. They were something he had
simply never seen before under the sun—and yet
the sun was still there in its accustomed place, and
as for him, he was there too, wasn't he? He existed.

He was alive—I'm alive, all right, he said to
himself, but then where am I?

He could see that he was standing right in the
middle of an immense waste of stone, and he
stared around with painful attention, trying to
get things sorted out inside his head.

From the other side of a long night—but am
I still in the same place? he wondered. Or have I
come out somewhere different, travelling that way
underground? Maybe finally I tunnelled right
under the mountain. How long did it last anyway?—from the other side of a long night he
remembered the same sun, but then the sun was
shining on beautiful green grass, on a wide rich
pasture where cows were scattered, where men
were working on the fields, carrying out manure
and spreading it. Everything was alive, the bells
tinkled on the necks of the animals, the men
called back and forth. . . . Silence. He looked:
no more men, no cows, no grass, no cabins. Stones
and more stones, and then more stones. In front
of him an immense field of rock sloped gently

away, right over to the other mountain range, the one that rose up on the south. He could recognize it now, yes, that was surely the southern range. At its foot something gleamed, and he couldn't think at first what it was. It was water, it was two little lakes.

They weren't here before. Where was he anyway?

He scratched his head again.

Every time he made a move the cloud of flies covering him flew up with a noise like a plucked violin string. Just the same, he told himself, I'm at Derborence sure enough. The valley is all changed, but the high places all around haven't. Below everything was different, up high it had all stayed the same. He began to name the peaks one after the other, as their names came back to him. Cheville up there, next the sharp peak of the Comb, the gorge down over there, the Woodcutter's Passage on the left. He turned a little, following the peaks, and tipped his head back to look up. Then he burst out laughing.

Because now he understood.

He turned all the way to the north. There was the glacier, nearly five thousand feet above under the peak of Saint Martin. The broken edge where the ice had fallen off was still fresh and gleamed in the sun.

He understood. He said to himself, "I see."

He nodded. "That's it. I understand. The mountain fell down."

It fell on us, he went on to himself. I can remember the noise it made and the roof flattening itself on the ground on one side.

He looked up. Easy enough to see the path it came down. Lord! what a drop, he thought. All the way down from up there and straight on top of us as if it had taken aim. No houses left of course —he looked around him at the vast expanse of tumbled stones stretching far off from where he stood in the middle—no, not a trace of grass, not a cow left, not a single man.

He said to himself, "Where are they?" and answered, "They must have already climbed out.

"But I was caught further underneath. I had to stay there.

"But now I'm out!" he went on. "It took me a long time, but I got out just the same."

Then he was happy. He saw only one thing: he was alive. He had eyes that could see, a mouth to take deep breaths of air, a body (he felt of it) to go where he wished, where he wished and as long as he felt like it.

He had a voice too. It was coming back to him. Now, when he thought of words, his tongue moved in his mouth and formed them. He had a voice then, a voice that travelled faster than he did and ran along ahead as a dog might to announce his coming.

He formed a sound in his throat and brought it out. It was still harsh and formless, but he heard it, he could hear himself, he had proved that he existed by that first shout of his, which the rocks echoed back again.

"Oh!"

And something answered, "Oh."

Then he called,

"It's me!"

"Me?"

"Me, Antoine Pont."

He called out his name and repeated it. He said, "The mountain fell down."

"The mountain fell on top of me, you see? But I got out from under it!"

He laughed out loud. Something laughed.

"You think it's funny?" he shouted. "I think it's funny too. Where are you?"

He got up.

It must have been nearly ten o'clock by then, for the sun was fairly high in the sky and it didn't appear in the valley until late. Before it could shine over the rim of the eastern mountains it had to climb a long way up the further slope, rising step by patient step to the summit.

Now it shone round and white in the sky. It was quite a good distance from the jagged rocks closing in the east, and its rays were already burning hot.

Antoine looked again to left and right, then turned toward the opening of the gorge and started in that direction through the tumbled rocks.

These were of all sizes and very unevenly distributed. Some were wedged into cracks between others that had fallen first, and a few of these even towered high above them, standing up above the flock of stones like a shepherd herding his sheep. Some stones were pointed and angular, some round, some tiny and mixed in with gravel and sand. In some places the rocks had fallen flat and were laid end to end in a continuous floor, while in others they were separated by big holes and cracks.

He had to go cautiously and pick his way, but he laughed with pleasure. Sometimes he sat down and slid. Sometimes, because of his broken shoes, he didn't move until he had carefully chosen the spot for his next step. Then he stopped and called,

"Where are you?"

He could still hear a faint formless sound. "You . . . ou . . . ouuuuuu . . ." then nothing at all.

By now he was not far from the bottom of the

landslide and on a level with one of the small lakes
which it had dammed up. At one end the water
overflowed into a little fall which splashed down
on the rocks and disappeared immediately.

He looked at the water admiringly because in
its depths the whole reflection of the mountain
could be seen, with a scrap of blue sky around its
summit, like a piece of cloth forgotten on wash
day.

He laughed. He laughed out loud. Then he
stopped, puzzled. "What?" he said to himself,
"nobody there any more? Hey! Halloa!"

He gave the call of the mountains, holding his
hands cupped around his mouth, "Halloa!" But
now there was no answer except a faint murmur
rising confusedly behind him among the rocks.

"Hey!" he called. "What have you gone so far
off for? Hey, listen, it's me . . . can you hear?
Antoine Pont. Halloa! Antoine . . ."

Nothing.

He began to laugh.

"They must have quit expecting me by now."

And he called loudly once more.

"Yes, sure, it's me! The mountain fell on me
but just the same I got myself out! Don't you believe me?"

Nothing.

"All right!" he called. "All right, I'm coming."

And he started off again, threading his way among the rocks. Here at the edge of the landslide were the biggest ones of all, enormous blocks of stone which had rolled so far from the rest that the grass was still growing between them. It was a beautiful green, soft and thick, paving the narrow alleys. For the cracks were like real alleys. They twisted and intersected, ran into dead ends or were half blocked up in the middle, and it was almost impossible for him to find his way in the confusion of passages.

It took him a long time, but with his buoyant high spirits he patiently unravelled the maze and kept steadily advancing.

Suddenly he appeared at the spot where the path began again beyond the rocks. It was the same old path, with the marks of mule shoes and hob-nailed boots printed deeply in the mud, the village path, oh! he recognized it all right!

Beside it flowed the stream, which had now found its way back to its former bed.

Yes, he knew where he was now. It was the same water, leaping and bounding down in its well-remembered way between the rocks that he remembered too.

He saw the old path, the path of the old days, plainly marked before him; all he had to do was follow it. Here we go! he thought. There was nothing to stop him any more. Before him were the first barberry bushes and the first pines, the former bordering the path, the latter standing up to right and left on the mountain slopes. Here we go! He began to sing, he waved his arms, he talked to himself. In less than a quarter of an hour he would be at Zamperon.

Ahead of him a little girl was pasturing a white goat along the path. She turned around when she heard him, stared, then began to scream and took to her heels, dropping the rope.

He laughed harder than ever.

"What's the matter with her? Hey . . ."

She disappeared around a bend in the path.

The goat had run away too and was leaping up the mountain in big bounds, the rope trailing after.

"You too! What's the matter with you? Hey there, goat!" he said.

But just then he turned the corner and saw three or four cabins before him. The door of one of them was open and over its uncovered chimney swayed a plume of white smoke as light and feathery as cattail down.

They must have made up the fire with wet wood.

A woman stood on the doorstep and somewhere he could hear the little girl still screaming. Then the woman turned to look at him.

Immediately she disappeared into the house.

She came out almost at once. The little girl was in her arms, her head covered with a corner of her mother's apron, and a boy of fourteen or fifteen followed them.

Antoine was still standing in the path, staring, when all three went off running as fast as they could. Then he started to run too.

At the doorway he paused and called, "Good day to everybody here, and good day, too, to everybody that isn't here."

Then he stepped into the big low room, shadowy and dark just now because the banked fire gave out no light.

"This is the Donneloye's, isn't it?" he asked. He looked around. "Hello! Nobody home?"

The room was empty. But what did he care? There was something good to eat hanging from the rafters. On a shelf stood butter and fresh bread. He broke the long loaf over his knee. He scooped butter out of the crock with his finger. There was a jug of milk too. A good thing they had all run away! He unhooked the dried meat—it was long and thin and not much bigger around than a sausage, with a hole in one end for a string—and bit right into it without waiting to cut any off. He drank, he ate; he ate and drank both together. His teeth champed noisily. He saw nothing any more, he heard nothing, he was closed to all impressions except the good taste in his mouth and the good warmth going down in his stomach and spreading through his body. He munched noisily, his stomach rumbled; after all those days, all those days on bread and water! And how many were there, anyway? he wondered. It was just like being in prison, only worse, because in prison there was light to see by, or at least a little. . . .

He didn't move. He was perfectly satisfied to stay right where he was, sitting on the bench with his elbows comfortably on the table. How good it felt! Then he said to himself, "Now what?" He couldn't remember where he was or why he was sitting there.

He pondered, then he nodded his head. Yes, sure, he said to himself, that was it, it was the mountain. The mountain? Yes, you remember. Well, time to get going again, then. He nodded again and said, "That's right, the mountain fell on me."

Suddenly he was frightened because the mountain was still close by.

Suppose it took a notion to fall again? If it started to fall . . .

"Still nobody here? Well, thanks just the same."

Banked with wet pine needles, the fire smouldered behind him on the hearth.

"Thanks very much."

His head was going round and round, but he could still see the path in front of him. He had come up from the right, hadn't he? Well, then, he thought, I need to turn left.

The birds began to gather along the stream, more and more of them as he walked along, until it seemed that there were two rivers, one running beside him, the other streaming by over his head.

There were magpies and jays and wood pigeons, and all the little twittering birds of the hedgerows and bushes. There were more and more of them, and their clamor grew louder and louder. "Yes," he kept saying to them, "yes, it's me. Yes, will you shut up!"

Then suddenly he was tired and let himself fall in a heap on the soft moss beside the path.

3

THAT EVENING Therese had gone to her mother's
garden, up the hill from the village and not very
far from the path to Derborence.

For she still lived, and the child within her
lived too. She had gone on living. She was up, she
went to and fro, she had even started to work
again.

There were eight widows and thirty-five father-
less children in the village now. They lived on, and
the children too. That's the way things are. The
tree split by lightning grows new bark. The broken
cherry tree covers its scar with white gum. The
hare with a broken paw has to go right on running.

She was only a little drawn and thin and in her
black clothes she looked pale under her tan.

She bent over, she straightened up. Every time
she leaned over she could feel the child in her
womb pressing heavily against her. She was growing bigger and bigger and lately the whole burden

had shifted and was rising higher in her body. It was cumbersome and uncomfortable.

All the time the child was there, saying, "Here I am!" so that she couldn't forget him, but this was no comfort to her.

For he has no father, she kept thinking. He will be all alone with me in life. She stopped working and straightened up for a minute. She tired easily these days and although still strong, got all out of breath after only a few strokes with the hoe.

"There will be only me to bring him up. Only a woman. . . ."

Night was beginning to fall. Twilight had come earlier than usual that evening, for the sky was lowering and threatened a storm.

Therese leaned on her hoe handle, looking in front of her where black clouds were gathering over the towering mountains to the west. The gorgeous sunset colors were swallowed up in darkness like a flaming torch suddenly extinguished in the sand.

A man went by below her on the path. Then a woman, hurrying to get home. Then there was nobody. She was alone, and the air darkened stealthily around her as if night were diffusing drop by drop in the cup of daylight.

The bushes along the slope were melting into

123

shadow from below. She could barely make out their faint outlines in the twilight.

It was time to go back, but she felt incapable of taking a step. She had no courage left to make any decisions, not even enough to move, and she stood still, leaning on her hoe, motionless under the dark sky. It was then that she thought she saw something. In front of her a vague whitish blur moved slightly behind the bushes.

Did she really see it? She remembered that in her condition it was easy to imagine things that were only inside her head. Your impressions were always a little confused. Women had longings, queer tastes for food, and found it difficult to tell the difference between what was actually happening and what they imagined.

She looked more attentively.

Something white moved again behind the bushes, fifty yards or so in front of her.

It seemed to have come from nowhere. It was just there, as if hanging in the air, because at that point the thick bushes hid everything below. Therese tried to be reasonable. She asked herself, "What can it be?" And thought, "It must be one of the neighbors." But a neighbor would have hobnailed boots that made a noise, while the shape over there was perfectly silent. It moved to one side, that was all, it moved and then became mo-

tionless. It looked for all the world like the top of
a scarecrow, a collection of rags and sticks set in
a garden to frighten the sparrows. Only this formless white thing kept on moving, shifting its position from time to time. And little by little, as
Therese stared, astonishment gave way to uneasiness, and uneasiness to fear. For the longer she
looked through the gathering darkness, the more
the impression grew that someone was looking
steadily back at her. The feeling grew stronger
and stronger. She didn't cry out, because she had
no breath left to call with, but she dropped her hoe
on the clods. She could hear her heart pounding,
like somebody knocking on a door. And the door
doesn't open, so you knock louder and louder.
. . . She waited, frozen, until the moment when
a hoarse voice came out of the night—but was it
really a voice? Guttural, formless, it sounded almost as if an animal was trying to talk.

"Unh . . . Unhhh . . ."

And yet there was a sort of speech in it too,
something like words, and it seemed to her that
somebody said, "Is that you, Therese?" But already she was running so fast that she could hear
nothing.

The lightning flashed, she ran. She ran, the
lightning flashed again. The grass sprang up in
front of her, suddenly a brilliant green with a

white thread of path running through it. Then there was no grass, no path.

She kept on running. Somebody was saying to her,

"Good Lord, what's the matter?"

In front of her the fire burned tranquilly on the kitchen hearth. She must have climbed the stairs without realizing it.

"Therese, what is it?"

But she dropped down on the bench without answering, pressing her tightly clasped hands between her knees.

From far off came a roll of thunder.

"Where's your basket? And the hoe?"

The lightning flashed again. Suddenly there was a window opposite her in the kitchen wall, then it was no longer there.

A blinding white square, it sprang into being, vanished, flashed out again, and with it Therese too was first brilliantly lighted, then swallowed up in darkness, then lighted up again.

First Philomene could see her leaning forward on the bench, then see nothing at all.

"Oh!" Therese said suddenly, "he'll get wet!"

Then she added, "If it really is he."

She paused.

"It is, and yet it isn't either. But then," she said, "they don't get wet anyway, do they? The rain goes right through them, poor things, and they can't feel the rain . . ."

In the returning flash of light she saw Philomene fling her hands up over her head, then drop them.

All the kitchen was bright as day, all the kitchen was blacked out by the night, the fire had time to glow redly before it vanished again.

"What are you talking about?"

"You know all right," said Therese without moving.

She paid no attention to the storm, nor even seemed to hear it, although it had now burst on them in a torrential downpour that thrummed on the roof like dancer's feet on the floor of a pavilion.

"You know what they're all saying. . . ."

She raised her voice as the rain redoubled its roar.

"Who?"

"The people from Zamperon, what they're saying about Plon, the shepherd."

Philomene shrugged her shoulders.

"No, he really knows things, Plon does," said Therese. "And he's lived a long time. . . . He says he can hear them at night. Because they're alive and yet not alive; they're on earth and yet not on earth."

"Don't be silly," said Philomene. "After all those masses we've had said? One every Sunday for your poor husband, and for Seraphin too?"

Therese shook her head. "I don't know," she said. "Maybe that isn't enough, because they weren't buried properly. How do we know? Maybe they have to have their purgatory there, where they died, because they didn't have the last sacraments. And so they wail and lament, and now they've come down to complain to us, to complain to me. . . ."

She spoke calmly. The storm was already moving off, behind the mountain.

The first downpour had passed, giving way to a steady fine rain. Once more the fire glowed, and the lamp shone tranquilly.

"They come down because they need us. Perhaps they can see us and recognize us, even though they're nothing more than a bit of thin air. . . . There may be one of them who misses me. . . ."

"What are you saying?"

"Oh," she said, "I don't know, only I was afraid of him because he doesn't weigh anything any more."

The lightning flashes came at longer intervals now, and were of a different color. They were passing away—did everything pass away? The storm

128

had gone, everything went away in the end. He had a body. Now he had it no longer.

"Listen," said Philomene, "suppose I went to fetch Maurice Nendaz?"

For now she, too, was beginning to feel frightened.

"We're only two women here," she said. "He might be able to tell us what to do."

She blew her nose and went to find her shawl, wrapping it well around her head and shoulders.

Therese said nothing.

Philomene went out; she still sat motionless, elbows on knees. On the roof the fine rain pattered delicately like the tiny feet of a multitude of birds.

There was no other sound. Then a cane knocked far down the street. Uneven footsteps climbed the stairs.

She didn't move.

A man's voice said, "What's all this story, Therese?"

"Oh," she said, holding her hands to her head and shaking it slowly, "just the same, I really did see . . ."

"Who?"

"Him."

"Where was that?" Nendaz asked.

"Up in the garden. It was all white, it didn't weigh anything at all. You know well enough what they're saying, what old Plon says. What do you think, Maurice Nendaz? Suppose they do come back after all! And they don't touch the ground because they don't weigh anything? There's no noise, it's like smoke, like a little cloud drifting around where it wants to go."

"Listen," said Nendaz, "I'll have to go and see. You said it was . . . ?"

"Yes," she said, "right close to the path."

"Well," he said, "don't worry too much. Maybe it's just your condition now and that's all there is to it. All you need to do is to shut the house up tight. And I tell you what, I'll just go up there and take a look. If I see anything, I'll come back and tell you. If there's nothing, I won't be back."

He asked, "All right?"

"Oh yes!" said Philomene, "that way we won't have to worry at all. . . ."

Therese said nothing, she still sat motionless, staring in front of her.

The sound of the cane receded into the night. . . .

4

N<small>EAR THE END</small> of the afternoon he opened his eyes. He had slept five hours at a stretch. He didn't know where he was any more. It was Antoine.

He looked around him. Evening was coming, he could see that, but what was he doing here all alone and why should he be down in the ravine?

He sat up on the moss, feeling chilly, for the sun had left him behind as it journeyed on over the mountains. He sat up and felt of himself all over, laying his hands on his legs and chest and asking himself, "Who's this?" Then he said, "It's me."

Satisfied, he stood up.

He was no longer sure where he was going, nor very sure where he had come from, because of the great confusion inside his head. But the birds had come back, and as they streamed by in greater and greater numbers they showed him the way to go.

Besides, there was the river that you could see if you leaned over.

Antoine followed the river, he went where the birds told him to go as their numbers kept on increasing.

And now there were no longer only the great somber birds of the mountaintops: the solitary eagle gliding endlessly above the cliffs; the hawk waiting on high to pounce on its prey cowering among the rocks; the black jackdaws with their yellow beaks, turning and fluttering around their nest on the face of the cliff.

Now there were smaller, tamer birds too, the little birds that greet you when you come down from the mountain; when you leave the rocks for the upland pastures, and the pastures for the forests. There were screaming jays, murmuring doves, and all the twittering birds of the hedges. They were green, gray and brown, some plain, some splashed with yellow, red or blue. Some wore collars or flashed one or two tail feathers of a different color. There were black and white magpies too—the further down he went the more birds flew up in front of him, showing that he was on the right path.

Antoine was happy to see them, and they seemed happy to see him, although timid too. The blackbird gave little frightened cries; others broke off their songs in the middle, and he called to them, "Stop! Wait for me, don't run off, where are you going?" He laughed with happiness as he greeted them, for they heralded the valley below, the good warmth, the abundance of bread and wine, a house, a real bed. . . . "Hello, there! Hey, wait a minute. Don't be afraid, it's me!"

He pushed his long hair away from his eyes and suddenly a part of his memory came back. "Say, that's right! It's me," he repeated. "The mountain fell down, but I escaped just the same."

And he began to run down the path, but he had to stop again almost immediately. The shreds of shoes on his feet had dried out as stiff as boards and hurt him. He sat down and saw that his feet were bleeding; they were the gray color of dried clay, with brown splotches on the skin. He took off his shoes or what was left of them, and threw them into the ravine.

Just there the walls of the gorge plunged to the bottom in a straight drop of more than two hundred yards, and the path, cut out of the rock, clung in mid-air to one side.

Now he could walk more comfortably, but in his bare feet he had to watch out for sharp-edged stones. The birds still fluttered up as he came, for there were more and more bushes and low shrubs as he came down the mountain.

"That's right, the mountain fell on me. And I've got a wife too.

"Only is she waiting for me still?" he asked himself.

He shook his head seriously over this thought as he walked along.

"And the others?" he wondered.

Still walking, he shook his head again.

The trouble was that he didn't know the answer to that. Nor to the other questions either. He realized that he didn't know anything. He knew only that he was a man named Antoine, who had been caught under a rockfall; who had got out, and so . . .

So what?

So he was going down the mountain.

He tried logic; why was he going down the mountain? To get home. Home: that meant a house, yes, and in that house there was a woman.

"In the house I'm going to there is a woman," he said aloud. "My wife. Let's see now, what is her name?"

It was no use; he would just have to learn everything over again. A whole world to be learned, the sky, the trees, the birds. . . . "Wait a minute, though," he said. "There's one I remember! It's easy, his tail jerks. Hey you!"

He waved at a wagtail in its somber coat balancing on the end of a branch and bobbing its tail, just as he had said, in quick nervous jerks. The birds were settling down for the night. Twilight was falling, and as he walked the walls of the gorge opened wider and wider on a darkening sky.

Then he went on as fast as he could.

"Hello, it's you!" he kept saying to the trees. "Yes, here you come. Hello! Here you are!" he said to the birds and the trees. "And here I come too. Me, Antoine. The mountain fell on me."

And he kept on walking until the path left the gorge and he could see opening widely before him the great valley in which flowed the Rhône.

He saw the Rhône; he said, "The mountain fell on me."

Who was he talking to? The Rhône. For the Rhône was down there in the valley, and he could see it. There was still enough light to see the river, all white and twisting like a snake among the stones, under the mountains whose great shoulders were piled high with clouds. He recognized it in the fading light and said to himself, "There it is, sure enough, so now I go left."

High up on the slope he turned to parallel the river, going upstream along the valley.

There was still enough light for him to see the shapes of the trees: the apple trees low and round, the pear trees pointed; apple trees like round balls, pear trees taller and reaching up to the sky. So it must be on the left, he thought. It couldn't be far off now. He looked to the left and, sure enough, there was the village, with its low slate roofs huddled together in a hollow on the slope so that it looked like a quarry (as in a sense it was, the work being the same: laboriously digging out the earth to get what was once underneath out on top).

He ran, he stopped to look, he ran again. He had left the path and was cutting across the slope.

In the twilight the air was warm and fragrant. It smelled of the essence of the earth distilled out all day by the hot sun, of dry grass, of the thyme and mint he walked on, all soft under his feet, of warm stones and the promise of the ripening wheat and the coming vintage.

He had left the path and was going between the bushes and the pines on the slope. It was then that he saw her, or thought he saw her, all dressed in black, standing there ahead. A woman. And isn't that the garden? he thought. Sure it is. I know it. Our own garden.

She bent down, she straightened up, she stood motionless.

It must be she. Who else? Of course it was!

He tried to call out, but then he was astonished at the strange sound of his voice. It was harsh and

136

formless, and it seemed impossible to drag it out of his throat, as if it were all covered with thorns scratching him and holding it back. He could hardly form the words at all.

He said, "Unhh . . . Unh . . ."

That was all.

"Hey! Wife!" he called.

All of a sudden there was nobody there at all.

"I didn't see a thing," Maurice Nendaz was saying. "Not a single thing."

It was the next morning.

"I was already there yesterday evening," he said, "because his poor wife was sure she had seen him."

He had got up before the dawn.

There he was with his cane, and Rebord beside him. He had gone to get Rebord, and Rebord had come down his wooden staircase.

A fine rain had fallen all night. It had stopped only a little while ago, and the clouds were low-hanging and sullen, a somber gray slab immovably fixed halfway up the mountain slopes on each side of the valley.

The two men kept looking up, but they could see nothing beyond the clouds.

"We'll have to go further up," Nendaz said.

"She says it was up by her garden that he showed himself."

"Huh!" said Rebord. "With the way it was raining last night!"

He was a bulky man and didn't look at all anxious to do any more climbing.

Nendaz was small and lean, and walked bent over his cane.

Rebord went on, "It's just nonsense!"

"Well, of course," said Nendaz. "But you can't reason with a woman. I promised her I'd go and look."

Behind them in the village lights were springing up in the windows, first one, then another further on, then still another. In the dark huddle of houses the tiny red dots looked like glowing cigar ends. And then, far down the valley to the east, the overhanging slab of cloud moved a little. It looked almost as if somebody had put a crowbar into the crack between the mountains and the clouds, and was heaving on the other end.

A heave: the slab of mist drew a little away from the mountains.

A heave: it rose higher, fell back again, then once more the clouds lifted. Suddenly the light slipped through the crack. Incredible, heavensent, a beam of sunlight streamed into the dark valley.

It was as if someone were lifting the slab of stone over a grave, and the silent dead felt life reaching out to them. Life reached out to death, and it quivered at the touch. A shaft of sunlight came up the valley like a lifted arm telling it to waken and live.

The roofs and chimneys of the village, with a few trails of faint smoke, could be seen in the pale light. Everybody had one cheek lighted up and the other still in shadow.

Nendaz had one cheek lighted up and so did Rebord.

"Rise," the light said to the valley. "Leave your slumber, depart from death."

And now, indeed, everything was stirring out of its deathlike sleep. The whole valley was coming to life. More lights sprang up, paling in the growing light. People coughed or blew their noses. Someone called; a door opened.

One more heave on the lever, far down the valley, and then the slab of mist came completely away from the mountain and split down the middle. Now the light did not come just from one side, but streamed down from overhead, and now each man saw his neighbor complete and whole, standing upright and ready for the day.

"Well?" said Rebord. "Can you make out any-thing?"

"Well . . ." said Nendaz. "Well, no. Not a thing."

From where they stood they could see all the hillside where the path winds up to Derborence. It lay before them in a semi-circle: first two or three gardens, then the slope steeply climbing higher and higher until it touched the sky. The returning light had given back color to the stones, pines and bushes on the hill and it shone out in gray, russet and black, slashed with green where the bushes grew in bands across the slope.

"Now . . ." said Rebord.

"Now what?" Nendaz asked.

"Now it's time to go back," said Rebord.

He didn't seem exactly reassured though, and hesitated a little. Then, since Nendaz made no move but kept on running his eyes back and forth searchingly over the hillside, he went on,

"It's all the fault of that old fool! Old Plon, the shepherd. He's turned all their heads, up at Zamperon. As if we hadn't done all we could, we others! All those offices, all those masses. . . . Wouldn't you think the least *they* could do would be to lie still?"

Nendaz inclined his head, that was all.

It happened that directly in front of the two men stood a little shed for storing hay, at the far edge of the fields and woodlots. It belonged to

Dionis Udry and just then they could see him leaving his house and heading toward the shed. He opened the door—it wasn't even locked, just on the latch. Then he pulled it toward him, but instead of going in he made a sudden move back. Then he leaned forward and tipped his head sidewise to peer in around the door.

He must have noticed the two men as he went by, for suddenly he turned toward Nendaz and waved at him to come over.

Nendaz put his foot and his cane forward together.

"You going over?" Rebord asked him.

"Of course I'm going over."

Nendaz started off. Rebord hesitated, then evidently decided to follow. But not very fast. He kept back of Nendaz and was at first a couple of yards behind, then three. Dionis waited for them without moving, and said, as Nendaz came up:

"Come and look at this. . . . Somebody slept here last night, come and look, quick! I haven't touched a thing."

In his turn, Nendaz looked through the crack in the door. The shed was three-quarters full of hay, sloping up from the door to the roof on the other side. And on the swelling slope, in the midst of a light mass of bristling, crisscrossing hay stems, there was one smooth place where the hay was

matted down like felt. It was like a mold of clay
still holding the imprint of a body.

"See that?" demanded Dionis. "What do you
know about that?"

Nendaz scratched the top of his ear.

"I don't know."

"Somebody must have made it, though?"

"Well, sure."

Suddenly they heard Rebord behind them.

"Lord! How do we know what's been going on!
But I know one thing. I'm going to get my gun."

It was Rebord who spread the alarm in the village, because as he went by he told everybody,
"Keep a good lookout, there's a robber prowling
around here."

He wouldn't listen to anybody, but climbed up
his wooden staircase and went into the house.
When he came out again he had an old musket
with a powder horn and a bag of bullets.

He sat down on one of the steps of his staircase,
and everybody could see him loading his gun:
pouring out powder, ramming it in and pushing
the rod down the barrel, while his wife, leaning
over from the top step, shouted at him:

"Don't go! Rebord, stay here! Rebord, do you
hear me? Don't go up there again!"

Some of his neighbors looked on without under-
standing what was happening.

By now it was full daylight. It looked as if it were going to be a fine day. The cloud ceiling was all crisscrossed with cracks like a piece of parched earth, and was lifting steadily along the mountain slopes. People could see a long way off now, and a long way up over their heads too, in the clear air, as transparent as a freshly washed window pane. The round drops on the leaves, all that was left of the night's rain, sparkled with multicolored fires in the sunlight. A cock burst out crowing again, opening his beak wide.

Then he appeared, far up the hillside, as if the crowing had called him out. Nendaz saw him first, and then Dionis, but they didn't realize what they were looking at.

It was three or four hundred yards away, and all white.

Something had come out from behind a bush, up by Therese's garden. It appeared, vanished, appeared again. It looked as if it were trying to hide, and yet trying to see at the same time. Then it disappeared again.

There it was, and coming closer.

Dionis began to back up, as if the closer the thing got to him, the less sure he felt of himself. Dionis backed up, so did Nendaz, and now the sun shone out brilliantly over the mountain, and then it, too, hid itself. The whole village was out by now. There was a hedge of people standing side by side just beyond the last houses. Everybody was there looking up the hill, and some of them saw nothing, some caught glimpses of what was coming, and others just thought they saw something. Nendaz and Dionis joined the others.

"Hey, see him?"

"No."

"There!"

"No."

"He's gone."

And another voice cried out, "No, there he is, over there now, back of the pine tree that burned!"

"Well, all I know," Dionis was saying, "is that somebody slept in my hay shed last night."

Suddenly a woman cried out, "Oh, I know well enough! I know what it is!"

Everybody asked her, "What?"

"It's the dead! The dead are walking! They're coming back and nobody will be able to stop them."

Somebody led her away.

But her words stayed behind, and as they ran through the crowd they began to take hold of people's imaginations. And with them came fear. For if it was really the dead coming back, who could stop them? How could they bar their houses against spirits who made nothing of doors or bolts?

One man went to get a pitchfork, another grabbed a stick, still another ran for his flail—only a few men there were, because of the dead up yonder, and some of the rest still away in the other mountain pastures. It was a summer village, full of women and children, with a few old men.

For a little while nobody could see anything; then all at once there was the white thing coming straight toward them. It had been hidden for a minute as it went through a thicket.

Some of the women ran away, others retreated to their staircases or doorsteps, making sure of a refuge in case of need.

Suddenly they heard a musket shot. Rebord had fired in the air.

Instantly the white thing disappeared.

Everybody fell on Rebord, crying out, "Good God, are you crazy? What do you think you're doing? How do we know who it is? Or *what*? You'll bring trouble on all of us!"

He shook his head, saying, "I only fired in the air. Besides, that's my business," he added.

He was already reloading his musket, paying no attention to anybody. Then he lifted his head. "Besides, look. It's gone."

He pointed up the hill. "There's nothing there any more. Nobody at all."

At that point Maurice Nendaz (who was a man

of sense) beckoned to Justin. He took him off to one side and spoke to him in a low voice.

Then Justin went off, running in the direction of Premier, the parish seat.

All this while people were talking and gesticulating, crying children who had been frightened by the shot were being taken home by their mothers, and everybody was pointing out to everybody else the hillside where nothing moved any more, where there was no longer anything living . . . living? Was living the right word to use, though? How did they know what the thing was made of? Did it weigh anything? Maybe it was nothing but air, one of those shapes that exist only to be looked at and then are nothing. Something that appears, disappears. . . . But suddenly a voice broke in on their babble.

"Where is he?" it said.

And it went on, "Who fired? Oh," it said, "you've frightened him! Now he won't come back for a while. . . . No!" somebody cried out, "no, let me alone!"

It was Therese.

"Because it's he, I know it is, it's he. Last night I couldn't be sure, because the night can trick you, but now that he's showed himself in broad daylight . . . now that you've all seen him. . . . Where is he?"

Nendaz held her back on one side, Dionis on the other.

"Where is he? I want to go and find him."

Philomene was there too, standing behind her daughter. Therese had a man on her left, one on her right, and she stood there a little in front of everybody, saying, "Let go of me!"

They tried to quiet her. "No, stay here. We don't know what it is. Besides," said Nendaz, "there isn't anything there any more. He's gone."

"Where was he, then?" she asked.

And then, "Oh, I know well enough where he was. I know better than any of you!"

She stopped struggling and stood perfectly still, apparently resigned to waiting with the others. Everybody looked up the hill again. Still nothing.

A gleam of pale sunlight touched the slope a moment, bringing out the colors. The trunks of the pine trees turned red, and a few stones sparkled in the light like window panes. Then the sun went behind the clouds again.

Everybody said, "Oh!"

With a sudden movement, Therese had broken away from the two men. She was no longer held, she was free and could go where she wanted to. She began to run straight in front of her. Nendaz limped behind, but was outdistanced because of his bad leg. She ran to the edge of the gardens, at the bottom of the hill where the rocks began, and stopped there all of a sudden.

She called:

"Antoine, Antoine! It's me . . ."

She said:

"Antoine! Is it really you?"

And then, far up the hill, everybody could see the white thing reappearing three hundred yards above, from behind a bush where it must have been hidden ever since the shot.

Somebody. Somebody with a man's body, but who no longer looked like a man, as she could see better than the others from where she stood. Somebody looking at her and hesitating.

And now she, too, hesitated. She tried to recognize him, but could not. He was a man, or something resembling a man, who had a beard and no eyes. He had a mouth—but could he talk with it? Did he have a voice? Something blackish flapped around his shoulders and the rest of his body was nearly naked and all gray like a stone. . . . A body like that of a dead man. . . . She backed away a little.

He still hadn't moved.

When Nendaz saw her hesitate he came up, tapping with his cane.

"Wait a little, Therese. Wait a little. We don't know yet, but we'll know better soon."

The bell in the chapel began to ring.

A shepherd was caught in the landslide at Derborence. He was imprisoned under the rocks nearly two months. He came back. Nobody could believe it. And just at that moment the chapel bell began to ring. All they had in the village was a small chapel where the priest from Premier came once a week to say mass. It was a little bell, with a clear high voice like a child's. The silver tone rang out, everybody heard it. It rose higher in the air and spread wider and wider over the valley until like a ripple reaching the bank and being returned, it struck the mountain wall and started back.

It travelled back, circling in the air over them like the hawk that people call the bird of good luck.

Then the priest from Premier, whom Justin had gone to fetch, appeared between the houses. He was black and white. In front of him he carried the Host, gleaming in the sun. A choirboy in red and white carried the cross.

They went by the fountain, and the people standing there knelt as they passed. Nobody was afraid any longer. They went on, the cross in front, the priest walking behind.

As they came closer to Therese she fell on her knees. While they passed she bowed her head, then she lifted it and followed the moving cross and the Host with her eyes. For now she would know. They would all know. If it was he, or only his shadow; if he was there in the flesh or only in the spirit; if it was her true husband who had come back to her, or only a homeless unshriven soul . . . . and the cross and the Host moved steadily up the hill to a point where the slope suddenly became steeper.

She joined her hands in front of her.

And he . . .

He took a step forward. He stopped. He had come out from behind his bush. He took a step forward, then stumbled to one side like a drunken man, and stopped again.

Are you a man? Are you a Christian? Are you a living being? He was trying to answer, everybody could see that. But it was too hard, he couldn't yet. He took a step. He stood motionless. He took another step.

"Is it you, Antoine Pont?"

Come, for we are all waiting, if it is really you. Our Lord waits for you, and the sign of his martyrdom. The wooden cross is held high before you. Is it really you, Antoine Pont, husband of Therese Maye, Christian, and son of Christians?

The bell rang on.

And now the man over there began to move again. He didn't stop any more, he came faster and faster; and from all the kneeling crowd came a long sigh, for he came facing the cross. And the cross began to gleam with light because of the full sunlight which suddenly shone out over the mountains.

The bell rang on.

And now he was bending lower. He bowed his head, his shoulders. Then, leaning far forward under the shadow of the cross, he flung himself on his knees.

5

SHE LOOKED at him across the kitchen and said, "Oh, Antoine, is it really you?"

He looked back at her.

"And you, is it really you?"

Then he burst out laughing and turned his back.

She had thought that he would be wild with joy. She had thought that he would come to her, put his hands on her head to hold her close, and never let her go. Oh, they would have so much to talk about, so much. . . . They would be standing up, she had imagined, or perhaps sitting down side by side. If they were standing, soon he would say, "Sit down Therese." And for long they would sit close together, each feeling the other's warmth, and talking softly back and forth. Then they would stop talking because there would no longer be any need for words.

Now here he was, and he had burst out laughing.

The kitchen was still steamy and full of the smell of soap. He had washed. They had brought him clean clothes and Rebord (who was something of a barber as well as a tavern keeper) had shaved him carefully and cut his hair.

Antoine was looking at himself in the mirror.

"Oh! What a small face I have!"

He looked again.

"Not much bigger than my fist. And," he went on, "a bad color. Not surprising though. You can just imagine . . . two months in a cellar! So," he went on, "Rebord wanted to shoot me, did he! Oh well, he's an old soldier, after all."

He turned away from the mirror.

"Look, there's a book! Your prayer book, isn't it?"

Therese was looking steadily at him, although still from a distance, as if she were afraid to come closer. And she asked again, "Oh, Antoine, is it really you?"

"Take a look. All you have to do is touch me. That's skin there, real flesh—and anyway, now that I've passed under the cross. . . . Come on and touch," he said. "You'll see for yourself. It won't disappear. It's solid, it lasts, it's me. . . ."

"Oh," she said, "is it possible?"

"Well . . ."

And he went on roaming around the room look-

ing at everything and naming objects as he came
to them.

"Hey!" he said. "There's that brooch I gave
you."

There was a crowd of people in front of the
house, but nobody dared come in. When Philomene, who was straightening up the kitchen, went
out to empty a pail of soapy water against the
wall, they pressed around her.

"Well, what about it?" they asked her. "Is it
really he?"

And again, "How is he, anyway?"

But just then Antoine opened a window under
which a little group of children had gathered, and
leaned out with a loud shout. He frightened the
children with his cry and his white face coming
suddenly out at them, and they scattered in all
directions, like a flock of starlings flying out from
the vines after a gun shot.

Antoine brought his head and shoulders back
into the room, laughing, and took up his tour of
the room again, checking things off as he came to
them and explaining, "You see, I've got to learn
everything all over again."

She wanted to go to him at last, take him in her
arms and hold him close. But she did not dare.

She had had so many things to tell him, but now

she could think of nothing. Her astonishment had put everything else out of her head.

She wanted to tell him, "Listen, I have a surprise for you. And it's a good surprise."

But he was saying, "Look, a chair! Say, that feels good."

He sat down on it and then laughed—why should he laugh? He laughed; then he began again, "Look, a pincushion! So you still sew, do you?"

Suddenly he asked, "What month is it now?"

She told him.

"And the day?"

Again she answered.

"And the date?"

He nodded.

"You see, that makes seven weeks less than everybody else that I've lived. Less than you. . . . But now," he said, "now that good times are back, I'll just have to catch up."

Somebody knocked on the kitchen door. It was the mayor, asking if Antoine could come over now, because the priest wanted to speak to him.

He was all ready. He had only to put his hat on. The people were standing in the street and around the door. He came out and they were all astonished to see him. Nobody could recognize him. "Oh, how thin he's got!" they said. "Is that really

Antoine? Can it be true? Lord, how thin he is!"

Still everybody pushed forward to press his hand, women, men, neighbors, even the timid and mistrustful children. He said nothing; he laughed at everybody. The mayor walked beside him. It was a lovely day, with only a little north wind blowing cool on one of his cheeks—the left one.

He walked beside the mayor and everybody else had to follow behind them because the street was so narrow. He walked unsteadily, still not very sure of his footing. Everybody was surprised to see him out in the open, so unused to the sun he seemed with his strange color like the white stems pushing up under dead leaves, or like the blanched vegetables that people grow in cellars away from the light. He said to the mayor, "I can't walk very well yet, you see, I've been under the stones so long. . . ."

"You'll manage better soon," said the mayor. "Anyway, we're almost there."

"It's just that I'm not under the stones any more." And he breathed deeply again, drinking in the air greedily. "Does it feel good!" He turned around to the others again and said, "It feels good, but it makes me dizzy."

He was in there for nearly an hour with the priest and the mayor.

Now it was in front of the mayor's house that

the people waited. They were already coming in from Premier as they heard the news, and soon there were more trousered legs than skirts among the waiting crowd. People asked, "What's he doing?" And the others answered, "They're asking him questions, in there."

When he came out, he said, "I'd better go and find my wife. I've barely seen her yet." But they all protested, "How about us?"

"She'll have all the time in the world to see you," they told him, "but we're just passing by. We'll have to go back soon. . . ."

Some of the men from Premier blocked his way. "Hello, there!"

"Is it really you?" they asked. "If it is you, you've certainly shrunk!"

As the people pressed forward, some who pushed up face to face with him edged away apprehensively instead of speaking. Others hung back behind the crowd and from a little distance found the courage to take a good look, noting his hands, his legs, and the clothes hanging loosely on what was left of his body (just like a scarecrow, he looked). From a distance they took note, too, of the deep hollows under his cheekbones, his cracked lips, his yellow teeth jutting out of his mouth—he was exactly like a corpse among living men.

"It simply isn't possible!"

People seemed to need not only their eyes, but their ears and fingers to make sure he was really there among them. They tried to get him to say something, they ran their hands over his clothes. Then they said, "Now, come along!"

Rebord took one of his arms, Dionis the other. And they led him over to Rebord's, saying, "We'll go and have a drink on this."

They helped him up the wooden staircase, making a great noise as they all climbed up. It was a wonder the stairs held. They groaned and tipped under the weight of men, but they all got in safely, all of them that could squeeze in, while the others stayed under the windows or went off to drink something in the neighboring houses.

They sat Antoine down facing the light at the end table and asked him, "Don't you want to eat something?"

"Come on and bring out some cheese and dried meat," they said to Rebord. "You certainly owe him that much."

Some of the others called out, "Where have you put your gun, you old fool? Hope it's stowed away safely. We don't want you pulling another of your fool stunts. . . ."

They said to Antoine, "Your health!"

Then they set their glasses down and looked at

him again. Newcomers were continually climbing up the stairs. Before coming in, each one went to the open window and took a good look at Antoine.

Some of them said nothing. They turned around and went quietly back down the staircase. But others couldn't keep still.

"Pont!"

Then he would lift his head and slowly turn toward them a wandering uncertain look, as if the light still hurt his eyes.

"Pont! It's you. Honest to God! Where have you been?"

They kept asking him, "How on earth did you manage to get out from underneath?"

The whole village was buzzing like an overturned beehive.

6

WAIT A BIT! he told them. "I haven't got things straight in my head yet. Where am I? Oh yes, I've come out from under the ground, and there you are, and here am I. All right!"

"Your health!"

"It's funny, because they've already asked me all this over at the mayor's house. Now I can't remember. . . . Everything comes and goes."

"Your health, Antoine!"

"And if you're finishing the harvest now, you'll have to explain things to me, because you hadn't even started haying when . . . wait a minute. Yes, that's right, you hadn't started yet. I remember. . . . What day is it? and the date? I already asked my wife that. Yes? What? The seventeenth of August, is it? The seventeenth of August, what year? You see I've lived so long away from years, from weeks, from days and nights. . . ."

They told him.

"Well, then," he said, "now we need to count up. I know I can't. You do it," he told Nendaz. "How many does it make?"

"Seven weeks, and even a bit more. It'll be eight weeks in a day or two."

"Lord!"

There he sat at the table, his glass before him, and everybody clustered around.

"You see, you get so you aren't used to daylight any more. You only see it once in a long while, a little bit, way up above. First it's there, then it isn't. Very far up there, between the stones. . . . The mountain fell down."

Through the open window the air flowed into the room. Wasps came in, too, and bees, and flies. All kinds of flies came in at the window. Some were blue and green; other little black ones made a cloud around people's heads. They looked like one of the black muslin veils that the beekeepers wear when they get honey from the hives. Antoine had one too; he sat there in it looking out at the others with his pale sunken eyes whose look seemed to meet theirs without really taking it in.

People came in, went out. The others shushed them, "Hey you, be quiet!" He paid no attention to anybody. He sat there, his look turned inward, as if he were following something going on there

161

behind his eyes, first one picture, then suddenly another one taking its place.

"Wait a bit, it's coming back . . . the mountain fell down."

He asked, "Could you hear the noise down here, when it fell?"

"Lord! I should think we did!" said Nendaz. "But we didn't know what it was. We would have thought it was a storm if it hadn't been such a fine night."

"A fine night, was it?"

"Lord yes! Stars all over, and not a cloud in the sky. So finally everybody went back to bed. Not me, though, ask Justin if I did. Because I said to myself, 'Maybe it's something else.' And I had my own idea what."

"I didn't hear a thing," said Antoine. "For me it wasn't the noise—too loud to hear, maybe. It was like a heavy knee pressing on my chest, and I fell right down from the wall, with the bed and the straw mattress. The bed, the mattress and me, there we were all three of us on the floor."

"Ssshh! Listen!" everybody said. "Shut up, you!"

This was to the man with the broken arm who was just coming in.

"For me," he said, "it was a beam coming down

162

on my shoulder. They fixed it up for me with splints. . . ."

But Antoine was going right on talking, "The point was the mountain had fallen—the mountain fell on me. And I lay there on the ground without moving, for I didn't know whether I could or not, you see, and anyway I didn't feel like moving just then. How long? Who could tell? And then, there was somebody. . . ."

It was as if he had just seen somebody, unexpectedly, there inside his head.

"And he called to me. . . . Yes."

But already he seemed to forget what he was talking about. Who was it? They didn't know. Antoine was already speaking of something else.

"That's the way you are, at a time like that," he was saying. "I was all taken up with the business of not moving. I didn't have the time to go take a look, lying there wondering whether I still had my arms and legs. For all I knew my back was broken. Somebody said, 'Where are you?' I said, 'Here.' And that was all. I lay there, and then, little by little, I began to move my right hand. First just the tips of my fingers, then the hand, then the arm up to the elbow, and finally my whole arm. . . ."

"Hello Antoine!" somebody said.

163

Two more men from Premier had just come in. Antoine didn't hear them.

"I thought to myself, 'Well, that makes one arm, anyway. Fine! Now let's take a look at the other one.' And with my right arm I went over to pay a visit to the left. . . ."

"Aren't you drinking?" they asked.

"Yes, I'm drinking. It's all right. And at the same time I lifted my left arm right up in the air. See? That was all right too!"

He laughed, and everybody laughed with him.

"Only now there were my two legs to find out about, and all the time I kept asking myself, 'Didn't somebody call me a while ago?' but anyway there was nothing any more. And I saw that I had one knee left, that made one. And another knee. Two! And both of them in good working order. I tried them out, lying there working my legs up and down like a little baby kicking on a bed when you take his clothes off."

People spoke to him, they asked him questions; he didn't hear them.

He was not governed by the outside world but from within, by the memories that came back to him, returning without order or sequence, so that at times he went ahead of himself, then suddenly was brought back to an earlier place in the story.

"Finally I was sitting up. Nothing was missing

anywhere about me. I had two arms, two legs and a body—not to mention my head of course . . . only do you know what? When I lifted my arm— I could lift it, you know. It was all right. Well, say, I lifted my arm up, and right there over my head, not three inches above it, there was a sort of ceiling: it was the mountain that had fallen down, it was a big slab of the mountain tilting up there right over my head. And I was caught in the angle underneath, just as if I was buried alive. . . . The twenty-third of June, you said it was? Yes, well, the twenty-third of June, near two o'clock in the morning maybe. Just about then. And I began yelling just as loud as I could, as if somebody could hear me. . . ."

He picked up his glass, and now it was he who said, "Your health! Your health too, Placide. You here too? Oh yes, you had your arm broken. And the others?"

There was a silence. But he forgot his question immediately.

"Oh! you certainly can be stupid at a time like that, can't you! At first I shouted just as hard as I could, but then I thought all of a sudden, 'I'd better not use too much air.' And I shut up. It struck me that there might not be much air left, and I started trying to breathe just as little as I could. I shut my mouth, tightened my lips, and just breathed through my nose, a little at a time, like this. . . ."

He sketched the gesture of pinching his nostrils together.

"Because you can just imagine, if I didn't have air. . . . To have to do without not only space and light, but air. . . ."

"How about food?" someone asked.

He said, "Wait."

"And water?"

"You're going too fast," he told them. "It's air that people need first of all, isn't it? It's much more important even than food or water. Right then I felt fine, because I could see pretty soon that there would be plenty of air, because of all the cracks there were between the stones. They were piled up to an enormous thickness overhead, but the whole heap was all full of cracks and holes that the air could get through. I could get along on all fours—there wasn't room to stand up—and I saw I had a chance, because the back wall of the cabin was still standing, there where it backed up against the solid rock.

"We'd already made two cheeses," he went on, "and we'd brought up enough bread to last us six weeks. And you can just imagine the luck, they'd landed on the right side for me, I mean right up against my rock, still on their shelf, so that when I felt along the rock with my hand . . ."

Everybody said, "Ah!" and Antoine nodded. "You understand? And I even had the mattress. . . ."

They understood. He went on.

They had to imagine, he told them, that the whole mass of the landslide was honeycombed, just like a sponge, with holes leading in all directions, only unfortunately the tunnels didn't always run into each other. One would suddenly come to a dead end, and although there might be another tunnel just a few inches away, there was nothing to be done, the way was blocked. For there might not be much distance between the end of one passage and the beginning of another, but what lay between was far stronger than any wall, being made of the same stuff all through, of solid stone, and all the same stone too. He would have needed gunpowder to budge it. They could just imagine the time he wasted on that sort of thing. They could count it up for themselves. Seven weeks!

He would follow up one crack, flat on his stomach, as far as he could, then, still lying flat, he would edge his way into another one, then perhaps he might be on his hands and knees, and the rock over his head would be slanting upward. . . .

He was still talking. "I'd be all encouraged when it started going up, for the daylight was overhead. But then, the next minute it would start sloping down, and I'd get discouraged again.

"It took time," he went on. "A day, two days— maybe three or even four, how could I tell how many? But do you begin to guess the trouble? Because I didn't have anything to drink. . . . My mouth was drying out as hard as horn, my lips were cracking, my tongue felt like a piece of leather and had swelled up so it wouldn't fit inside my mouth any more. Finally I came back and lay down on the mattress, telling myself, 'You'd better lie still.' You just don't know how lucky you are, up here, with your clocks on the wall, the whole sky overhead, and I kept saying to myself, 'What luck they have, with their fountains—their beautiful fountains—and their springs flowing right out on top of the ground. And here I am, if I could only have just one little drop of water, oozing out from time to time at the end of a bit of moss!'

"Plop."

What was that sound?

They were at Rebord's, the room was full of people; Antoine lifted his finger, "Plop. . . ."

It was like a slowly swinging pendulum at first. Then faster, faster. . . . "Plop . . plop . . plop!"

He got up from his mattress and crawled forward, holding his hands out in front of him. And all of a sudden he raised his head and the water came running down over his face.

"It was the runoff from the glacier. It had been all dammed up by the landslide, and now it was finding its way out between the rocks; one trickle had come over as far as my crack. It was just like a little hanging string and I could feel it moving and alive between my hands when I raised them up straight. There it was, it was alive, and I was going to live too, because of it, and quick quick I went to get a bucket to catch it in, because I thought, 'If it should ever stop, now. . . .' And there I was—saved! Because now I had everything, you understand, everything a man needs to live. Something to eat, to drink, to breathe, to sleep on. . . . All I had to do now was use the time I had—and plenty of that too, wasn't there? I was certainly going to have all the time I needed, we can see that now, can't we? Seven weeks, and even more than seven weeks. . . ."

All the afternoon it went on like that, at Rebord's.

New arrivals kept coming in and interrupting him. People asked him questions or proposed his health, and he would have to stop to answer them, or drink another glass.

But each time he would go back to his story.

"The cracks were just like the drains they have under the roads. Mostly they were so narrow I'd rub against them on both sides when I crawled through. Where I could see the walls I'd made marks on them so I could find my way back, but where there wasn't any light at all I'd just have to go back and forth, over and over, until I learned the way by heart. Sometimes I'd go a long way in one direction, then the passage would come to a dead end, blocked up solid, and I'd have to go back on my tracks. Sometimes it would be right over my head that I could see a faint gleam of light. I'd try to climb straight up to it, like a chimney sweeper. Up . . . and up. . . . Then suddenly I'd see a slab of rock sticking right out across the crack. No good, I'd have to climb down again. Then I'd see some light over to the left and I'd start off again toward it, just like a plant growing toward the light: that first shoot from the seed that's as delicate and thin as thread, and as strong as a bar of iron. But I didn't have the equipment a plant has, nor its power either, for I kept going first in one direction and then in another, on the track of ideas that would turn out to be no good. Seven weeks of that! Sticking to it was what it took. And caution too, because sometimes the crack I was in would be all choked up with small stones and rubble, and I'd have to clear it out very carefully, working with just the tips of my fingers, very slowly, and stopping to test the ceiling every few minutes—you can imagine the time it took."

And he went on, "Seven weeks!"

Twilight was beginning to fall.

"Well, anyway," they said, "here you are, finally."

They looked him over. "And you look better already. Anybody can see that you're getting your strength back . . ."

They all looked at him as he sat facing the evening light. There was a little color in his cheeks now.

"The wine's fixing you up, you had too much water to drink! Hey, Rebord, bring him another glass! Yes, see there, right up on his cheekbones. . . . Your health. Your good health, Antoine!"

But this time he didn't drink. He was thinking, his hand still curved around his untouched glass.

Suddenly he asked, "How many of us were there?"

"Where?"

"Up there."

There was a silence. Then someone said, "Well, let's see. Twenty . . . ?"

"Eighteen," said another. They looked at Antoine.

He asked, "How many came back?"

They could hear the birds twittering in the trees outside.

Finally someone said, "Well, there's you. . . ."

"And Barthelemy," they added.

"Barthelemy?" Antoine asked. "Where's he?"

"Listen," said Nendaz. "You're all tired out. We'll talk about that another time, if you don't mind. . . ."

Antoine paid no attention.

"Where is Barthelemy?" he asked again.

"Well," said Nendaz, "poor Barthelemy. . . . Well, it was just his hard luck," said Nendaz. "He got pinned under a rock."

"And then?"

"Then?" said Nendaz. "Well, then . . . you see. . . ."

"Yes," said Antoine, "I see all right. I was up there. I know what it was like. It comes down on you and nothing can stand up to it. And I understand too, the others, all the others . . . Jean Baptiste and his son, the two Mayes, all the Carrupts, Defayes, Bruchez . . . I understand all right, but . . ."

He brought his fist down on the table. "But one of them isn't dead! Lord," he said, "I'd forgotten! He's alive still, I tell you. . . . When the mountain fell. . . . It's my fault," he said, "I had forgotten all about it."

Once again they could hear the birds chirping in the trees outside.

And Antoine could see him; he said no more, because he saw. He was silent, staring fixedly before him. He saw a man already old and wizened, his small light eyes, with no eyebrows, sunk deeply in his head. They were sitting together before the fire, near nine o'clock in the evening. And then . . .

He brought his fist down on the table again.

"He's alive, I tell you! He's alive, because he called to me. I was on the ground with the mattress. He was my friend, you understand. More than a friend. He was like a father . . ."

The people around him were still silent.

"Without him I would never have got married. I couldn't have managed it. . . . Well, then, he's alive," he said. "He called out to me while I was lying on the ground. He said, 'Hey, Antoine?' I wanted to answer, I didn't have any voice left. 'Hey, Antoine, are you there?' I wanted to say yes, but nothing came . . . I must have passed out. But he's up there still, and he's alive . . . Seraphin."

Nobody said anything. And he went on.
"All we have to do is to go and find him."

All day long there were women in Therese's
house. Every minute somebody was knocking at
the door: people come to hear the news, or neighbors who expected to find Antoine at home. She
had to keep telling them, "He isn't here."

"No," she would say, "he had to go over to the
mayor's house to talk to the mayor and the priest."

Then, as the afternoon wore away, "No, he isn't
back yet. I imagine you'll find him over at
Rebord's. He's with friends, they've probably
stopped in to have a drink. . . ."

(It's funny, because I'm his wife, after all.)

Philomene sat before the fire. She kept shaking
her head and saying, "It's great good fortune."

"What luck!" all the visitors said. "To find
your husband, and your son-in-law, after seven
weeks!"

"Yes," agreed Philomene. "It's great good
fortune. Only," she would add, "there's misfortune in it too, for he wasn't alone up there, but
he's alone to come back. There were two of them.
My poor brother!"

She crossed herself.

"My poor brother! It's as if he had died all over again."

And then it was eight o'clock in the evening. Little by little everybody had gone home. Finally Philomene left too. Antoine was still not back. Had he forgotten her? Did he even remember that he was married? "He didn't notice a thing," she thought. "And me three months along already."

She looked at herself in the mirror, standing sidewise so that the light fell on the front of her body.

"It shows," she thought. "Anybody could see it, especially with my new dress on. It's tight around the waist already. Just the same, he didn't notice a thing. . . ."

She lingered a little longer, waiting. The lamp shed a soft glow of light on the freshly made bed. His evening meal was ready on the kitchen table. He did not come.

"I'm going to look for him."

She went as far as the door and pulled it open. The stars were out already in the evening sky. Then she thought of her neighbors, of the men probably still with Antoine, and her courage failed her.

They would laugh at her. So you're running after your husband already, are you? they would say. Let him alone, for goodness' sakes! He's found some friends to be with, what could be more natural? Let them have a glass together. He'll be back. Give him time.

That's what they would all say, and after all, weren't they right? "No," she said to herself. "I'll wait. Let him come as late as he wants to, at least he'll find me here. I'll sit in the kitchen, so he can see me the first thing, waiting faithfully. . . ."

She sat down by the fire with her hands quietly in her lap, and did not move again.

Then, finally, there was a sound of voices in the distance, far off, but clearly heard in the silent village. They were men's voices, there must have been several; a whole group of men.

They came closer, she could hear someone saying, "All right, we'll leave you now."

Then came Nendaz' voice, "Good night, Antoine."

And another, "We'll be seeing you."

Then, "Good night . . . look out, there's a step there . . . All right? Good night."

The steps came nearer. The steps were climbing the stairs, and stumbling over them. They stopped for a moment before the door.

A hand fumbled for the latch.

And Therese? Therese stood up. As she had planned, she stood before him, so that she was the first thing he saw when he opened the door. He stopped, surprised.

"Hey!"

He looked at her. "Hey, that's right! It's you, isn't it? Yes," he went on to himself, "I've got a wife . . ."

He passed his hand over his face.

"If that was all!"

She said, "Antoine!"

"Your name is Therese. See? I remember! And we're married too, only . . . I have to . . . before . . ."

"Antoine!" she said. "Antoine!"

"Where are my work clothes? You see, he's alive, really. Over at Rebord's they didn't believe me. I've got to go and find him."

He had come forward, he looked all around him, then stood still, swaying. He was like an uprooted plant, a tree sawed through at the base. He had to hold on to the door frame to get into the bedroom.

"No, he isn't dead, it's just the way I told them. He isn't dead, because he called to me. . . . He just can't get out, that's all. He's still caught there under the rocks."

She could find nothing to say. The light shone softly over the big bed with its turned-down sheet. He was muttering to himself.

"Could they be in the closet, maybe?"

He got over as far as the bed, then suddenly toppled over sidewise, as if he had been hit on the head.

He fell half on the bed, his face and arms on the covers, his legs trailing on the floor.

He was asleep, he must have fallen asleep the minute he fell, and there was no waking him. Therese took off his shoes and coat, she pulled him up on the bed and turned him over on his back; he felt nothing, he let her do what she would, limp and docile as a dead man with the warmth of life still clinging to him.

He slept with his arms thrown out, his mouth half open. And as he slept he snored, with a raucous, regular, unnerving sound as if someone were rasping wood. Therese stood looking down at him. But the snores were too much for her. Bewildered and heartsick as she was by the events of the day, she simply did not have the courage to do her duty as a wife and lie down beside him.

She spent the night at her mother's.

7

HER NEIGHBORS saw her coming down the street from her mother's the next morning.

"Are you out already?"

They were taken aback to find that she hadn't spent the night with her husband. But then, since the thing was done . . . "You've come too early, anyway. You'll have to let him have his sleep out. Men that are as tired as that, why you hear of them sleeping three days sometimes . . . yes, three days and three nights at a stretch."

The morning was already well along, though. It was nearly nine o'clock.

Then, since Therese hesitated before going in, "Go on! Go on in!" they encouraged her. "If he's still asleep you won't bother him any, and if he's awake already it probably won't exactly upset him to have you join him. . . ."

They were still laughing as Therese went in the

door. She disappeared inside. Then suddenly there she was again.

"Oh God! Oh God!"

"What's happened?"

"Haven't you seen him?"

"Who?"

"Antoine."

"No."

"Oh God! He's gone!"

"Oh well, if that's all!" they said. "You had us scared for a minute. He's probably just stepped out. All you need to do is to look around, he must be somewhere in the village."

But Therese shook her head. And once started, she kept on shaking it senselessly, as if she had forgotten how to stop.

"No," she said, "I know where he is. He's gone back."

"Back? Where?"

"Up there."

It was just then that two men showed up from the valley, an official from the county court, and a gendarme. They had come to take Antoine's deposition. When they inquired in the village, his house had been pointed out to them, and as they approached it they saw a woman at the top of the steps. She was shaking her head and gesticulating frantically, and when she saw them she burst into wild laughter.

"Look, here's the Law coming! And a fine time you picked to show up, you did! A fine time . . ."

But all at once she changed her tone. "Oh, please hurry and go up after him!" she begged. "If he is up there . . . oh, please! Nobody knows what might happen!"

Therese was right; he was on the mountain.

He had started before dawn, retracing his previous journey and showing up finally in his new suit and white shirt at Biollaz' cabin. It was not far from the place where the great stones began —those stones which nowadays the moss covers with old gold, soft yellow, gray on gray, or dark green—just a little in front of the landslide where the biggest blocks, the ones that look like houses, now have all kinds of bushes growing in the cracks and fissures of their sides: barberries, huckleberries—sturdy little mountain shrubs, with thick leaves and glossy berries.

He stuck his head through the door.

"Anybody home?"

He asked, "Don't you know me?"

"No, I can't say I do."

"Antoine."

"Antoine what? There are lots of Antoines around here."

"Antoine . . . look a little closer, can't you? Antoine Pont, from Aire!"

"Good God!"

Biollaz backed away.

He stood a little distance off, staring fixedly at Antoine's face, entirely visible now he had taken his hat off. He tried to think how it would look with a more healthy color, a different shape. . . . He imagined it rounded out, ruddy. . . . "Say, wait a minute . . . By God, it is! It is you! Where did you come from?"

Antoine said, "From underneath."

He pointed; it was close by.

"I was caught under the rocks like the others; only I got out finally."

"Impossible!" Biollaz was saying.

And he went on, "How did you manage?"

"Crawling on my stomach, on my hands and knees. . . . Seven weeks."

"And just now, where are you from?"

"The village."

"Loutre!"

Biollaz began to shout.

"Hey, Loutre! Come on over!"

Loutre was working close by. He came over.

"Do you know who that is?"

Loutre stopped a little distance away. He looked uneasy.

"No."

"And yet you know him well enough. You must have seen his brand many's the time. A. P. ...."

"Whoever he is," said Loutre, "he's got more skin on his neck than he needs."

"Take it off."

"And he sure needs flesh on his cheeks."

"Plump them up."

"Pont!"

"That's it! See, you can come closer, it's all right."

Loutre came closer. And now he too asked, "Where are you from?"

Once more Antoine pointed toward the north, where the mountain towered up and the bottom of the great pile of rocks was just visible around the corner. He began to tell his story again, but Biollaz was asking, "When was it?"

"Yesterday . . . no, the day before."

Biollaz shouted again, "Marie!"

Donneloye's wife lived close by, in one of the neighboring cabins. She came to the door, then stopped as she saw them. Biollaz called over to her from where he stood, "Look, Marie, do you remember the ghost you saw day before yesterday? When you ran away? Remember what a good appetite it had, and what a capacity for food? Well, here's your ghost right here."

"Really?" she said. "Who is it?"

"Antoine Pont."

Dsozet was standing beside his mother now, poking his head out to see better.

"Yes, it was me," Antoine said. "But you see I was hungry. Just imagine, seven weeks! And I know I couldn't have been much to look at. But it's really me, I promise you, it's me," he went on to her, "and I'll pay you what I owe you for the food of course."

Donneloye's wife took a step or two outside the house.

Antoine was going on with his story. "And after I left your place, I went on down to the village— and I had to convince them it was really me, too, before they let me in. At first they were like you —they even shot at me. They thought I must be a spirit. We all drank together," he went on. "They brought the priest over from Premier," Antoine said, "and then we all sat down and drank together."

Dsozet had come over too, and was listening with the rest.

"Only you see," Antoine explained, "one of them is still up there; it's because of him that I have to go back up. You haven't seen anybody

else around, have you? I started before dawn, because I knew if anybody saw me in the village,
they'd try to stop me. They keep trying to tell me
that there's nobody left. But I know one of them
is . . . you haven't seen him?"

Now there were quite a few men standing
around Antoine and listening without understand-
ing very well what he was talking about.

"Because he isn't dead . . . Seraphin, you remember him . . . Seraphin Carrupt; quite an
old man, yes, sure, you know. That's who I mean.
He's my mother-in-law's brother, and if Therese
and I finally got married it was because he helped
us. For at first my mother-in-law didn't want me
in the family at all. So you see, he's an old friend
—more than a friend. . . ."

"And he's still there . . ." he went on.

"Where?"

"Up there . . . we were together in the cabin
when the mountain fell. Oh, I remember all right,
now. We were sitting before the fire. He said,
'You're lonesome, aren't you?' He said, 'Or do I
count for nothing?' Much more than a friend,
like a father really. You know I'm an orphan.
Well, I got out all right, but he's still up there
under the rocks. I told them all that in the village, but they didn't believe me, that's why I had
to come back. I'm all alone, but you can help me.

How many of you are there? At least ten. We can do it. He's alive, I tell you, I remember perfectly. I was lying on the ground and he spoke to me. He said, 'Where are you, Antoine?' Only he hasn't found the right way out yet."

The listening men stirred and murmured. "It just doesn't seem possible!" they told him. "How could he be alive, after all that time?"

"How about me? I was in there seven weeks. It would only be a day or two more for him. Look, will you come? But of course you will. We'll try to call him. Or maybe it would be better to get hold of a gun and fire it off. Then he'd know what direction to head for. . . ."

He talked more and more wildly, very fast, never pausing for an answer to his questions, his words tumbling out confusedly in his haste. The men gathered around him listened in silence and shook their heads dubiously. But finally two of them, Biollaz and Loutre, decided to go with him.

The three men climbed up to the right of the rocks, by a path which brought them quickly to the slope high above it. With each step up the steep incline, the great pile of stones seemed to sink down beside them as if it were being lowered on a rope. Instead of a heaped-up mound, it soon began to look flat; finally the big blocks looked like gravel, the little ones like sand.

At first there was only one ridge in front of them, hiding the further slope with its crest like an upflung wave against the skyline. Then the next ridge came into view, at first high above them, then lower and lower as they climbed, until suddenly there was nothing in front of them but air, and they could look out. "Good Lord!" said Antoine.

"Yes," said the others, "and you should have seen how it smoked, too."

"Smoked?"

"Of course. All that dust! For three days you couldn't see a thing."

But now they could see everything. Everything in the great hollow was clear and distinct, and in the silence the slightest noise was audible. The only sound was their nailed boots striking against the rocks with a sound like a dog crunching a bone. Then that, too, ceased and the silence was unbroken as they reached a sort of terrace on the edge of the cliff and stopped climbing. Antoine looked out over the great sweep of tumbled rocks and shook his head.

"To think that I got out of that alive!"

And he went on, "But if I got out alive, then he can too."

He looked again at the enormous catastrophe below, like a turbulent sea struck suddenly into stone—at all the barren waste of rocks where not a living thing remained. Then he said, "He's there."

Everything was dead, but Antoine said, "He's alive." And yet strain their eyes as they would, they could see nothing moving anywhere in all that space, whether on the sparkling surface of the rocks, in the dull patches of shadow between them, or even in the air above. Not a bird, that morning, wheeled overhead on its great wings, or fluttered with strident calls in front of a crack in the cliff. Everything was dead. But Antoine said, "He is alive."

He pointed. "Look, do you see those two big blocks? Down there? Well, that's where I came out. And the cabin . . . the cabin must have been a little lower down the mountain from that. But where?" He shook his head. "Lord! It's hard to see where anything was in all that mess. . . . First I'll have to get my bearings, and it isn't easy. Where's north? Over there, is it? In that case," he said, "I've got it. It must be that steep pitch in the rocks over there. They're tipped up because the cabin was backed up against a ledge and the rocks went down over it. He must be there. But how to find it when I'm down below. . . . I'll have to figure out the way and keep it in my head if I don't want to get lost. Yes, that's it! Seraphin . . ."

He shouted.

"Seraphin!"

He called with all his strength, his hands cupped around his lips, and the three syllables of the name rang out separately, like a trumpet call, into the vast ocean of air around them. He shouted, and so slowly did the sound travel that at first it seemed to vanish, to have been swallowed up and lost completely in the tranquil air. Then the echo came back to them from the other wall, the first time clear and almost intact, the second a little muffled and blurred on the edges, and the third no more than a faint murmur, like the rustle of a light cloth trailed behind you through the high grass.

"What we really need," Antoine said, "is a gun. But surely you've got a pickaxe and a shovel you could lend me . . . ?"

8

TOWARD EVENING young Dsozet turned up in
Aire. He told everybody, "Yes, he's up there all
right. But . . ." and he shook his head and pointed to his forehead.

"And Dionis with the gendarme?"

For they, too, had set off that morning for Derborence.

"Of course!" Dsozet said. "They're up there
too; it was them that sent me down here."

"Sent you down? Why?"

"Because Antoine won't come back. He says he
won't come down again without Seraphin. . . ."

"What's he doing?"

Dsozet screwed up his face and touched his forehead again with the tip of his finger.

Something stirred in Therese's heart. "I'll have
to go after him, then," she said. "Because of the
child."

"What are you thinking of?" protested Dsozet.

"Why, he's got himself a pick and shovel and he keeps saying Seraphin is there under the rocks and still alive. He says he heard Seraphin call to him. And some of the men started to go with him, but they came right back down."

"Why?"

"Because they were afraid."

"What of?"

"They were afraid of the shepherd."

"What shepherd?"

"The one with the flock of sheep up there."

"Oh, Plon."

"Yes, the one that pastures along the Dubonere. Well, he turns up there with his flock. He gets up on a rock. And he says, 'Don't go any further.' "

The men nodded. "Yes, old Plon . . . he knows things, up there on the mountain. . . ."

"Yes, that's the point, and then when you start to go by him he shouts, 'No further!' and everybody is afraid to go on."

"And Antoine?"

"Oh, him! He went on just the same. He's got nothing to lose."

The listening men nodded soberly again.

"Plon says he's just a semblance."

"Who?"

"Antoine. Plon says he isn't real at all, that he's only a spirit. Sure, I know you can see him,

but maybe it isn't a real body you can see . . .
not like ours. . . . And Plon says the reason he
came down was to toll some of us back up there
to the others, because they're unhappy and jealous of us, and need company up there under the
rocks. . . ."

The men stirred uneasily. "What do you suppose we'd better do, then?" they asked each other.

Therese stood in the crowd. She did not hear
the others talking, she was listening to a voice
speaking in her heart, saying, "Therese, go and
find him."

The voice said, "Thoughtless woman, did you
tell him what must be told at the right time, the
good time, the time when it was needed? Did you
even try to keep him with you, by staying with
him through those hours of the night that trick
men's thoughts? And yet the cross must have
shown you that it was really he. Or didn't you
believe? Have you forgotten that you and he are
one flesh, woman with no memory?"

The men had gone off to Rebord's to stand Dsozet a drink, although he was hardly the right age
for it yet. Therese walked home slowly. The voice
was still speaking. "Repair your mistake now. Go,
woman, find your husband. Go; find the right
words, find all the words you need to make him
understand, to make him come back. Wake him,

for he is numb with sleep. Go toward him with your secret, go and say to him, 'We are three. There is a child coming, and he will need you.' "

They were drinking with Dsozet at Rebord's and telling him, "You'd better sleep here tonight, and then tomorrow morning we'll see what can be done."

Therese thought, "I'll go tomorrow morning."

She called to her mother who sat weeping in the kitchen.

"I'm going up," she said.

"Where?"

"Up there."

"Oh!" said Philomene. "Oh, Therese!"

But Therese went on, "Could you fix up a basket for me to carry? Put a white cloth in it, and two bottles of the good wine. And everything you need to make a good meal, because it's for him, and I don't imagine he has any too much to eat up there. Some ham, and the fresh bread, will you, Mother? And then fold the cloth back over the top, so it will look nice."

"You're really going up there?"

"Of course."

"But why . . . ?"

"So our child will have a father."

While she talked she was getting ready to go out. That evening, however, she did not go far.

Nobody had gone to bed yet. They were all out on their doorsteps, in little groups at the top of the staircases, talking things over. When they saw Therese coming they stopped and fell silent. The alley was already darkening into night as she walked down it. Here and there in the dusk she could see a bright red glow where a door stood open, with perhaps the black silhouette of a head outlined against it and nodding downward, or the outline of a shoulder leaning a little forward and to one side. The people fell silent as she passed. She said, good evening, and they replied, good evening.

She went on until she came to Rebord's house.

As she climbed the steep wooden staircase her feet rang hollowly on the steps. But they were talking so loudly inside that nobody heard her. She knew well enough what she was doing. It was never the custom in the village for women to go into a tavern. And Therese didn't actually go inside. She stopped before she came to the door and looked through the window there. It opened right over the staircase so that anybody standing on the stairs showed only the top of his head and his eyes at the window, making it a convenient place to see without being seen. Therese looked through the window. Yes, he was there, she had thought he would be. Nendaz was sitting with the others.

He was there, and young Dsozet with a drink in front of him, although he was hardly old enough for it, and Rebord too, and the mayor, and all the men from Premier.

She stood on the stairs, and called through the window.

All that showed above the sill was the top of her head and her eyes. She was out in the night, in half-darkness; her hair was black, her forehead white, her eyes black, and she called, "Nendaz! Nendaz!" He didn't hear her at first, because of the noise and because his back was turned to the window. Then he turned around all of a sudden.

And one by one the noisy voices of the men talking tumbled into silence like sticks of wood falling off one of those piles of cordwood people stack up for the winter in their sheds.

"Nendaz, could you come out here a minute?"

Everybody looked in her direction, but she had already disappeared.

Nendaz got up. Nendaz leaned on his cane, he limped out to the landing and down the stairs.

Therese was waiting for him.

"Nendaz," she asked him, "couldn't you come up with me?"

"Where?"

"Up there."

"What for?"

"To look for him. . . ."

"Well . . . now . . ." said Nendaz uncomfortably.

For he could see well enough that probably she was set on going, no matter what he said. He felt embarrassed. After all, it wasn't right to let a woman go by herself on the road, least of all a road like this one, solitary, dangerous, never ending.

He scratched his ear. Then he said, "Well, when do you want to start?"

"Early tomorrow morning."

9

THE MEN were already in the fields, hurrying to get the rye harvested. As they worked they hardly had to lean over at all; on the steep slopes the bottom of the next row of grain was practically on a level with their sickles.

Where they had already passed, the sheaves stood up three by three, leaning toward each other and tied together at the top. In the faint light of early dawn they looked from a distance like little old women gossiping with their heads together.

Dsozet had come along with Therese and Nendaz, to have company on his way back to Zamperon.

It was a calm and hazy morning. The air was the color of ripe wheat and the same soft color stretched off below them and to the left, where the morning mist still filled all the hollow of the great valley which they could not see. But from its hidden depths a voice rose up to them—a voice telling an old, old story that had no end, and perhaps had never had a beginning. It was the Rhône that they could not see, it was the Rhône that they heard.

For the Rhône has always been there, and from time immemorial it has mumbled in the valley, raising its voice through the night, lowering it to a faint murmur as the light becomes stronger and day comes.

Therese walked quickly, and so did Dsozet who was still young and energetic. Nendaz had trouble keeping up with them and ground the iron tip of his cane down on the pebbles with each step.

Something was pulling Therese forward as she climbed. There she was on the path, her basket on her arm. And now she could be seen from a long way off, for the soft golden haze around them (that light mist that heralds a fine day in summer, and later on is the first harbinger of approaching autumn) was thinning out and shredding away into nothing, although there was not a breath of wind. It did not lift or blow away. Rather it seemed to be settling, as if it had been a solution of fine powder in the great bowl of air around them, a powder that was now imperceptibly sinking down and coming to rest on the bottom.

Therese was pulled forward by something. She said nothing, the men said nothing. Nendaz was bent over his cane. High over their heads the mountains were beginning to sparkle as the sky became more and more transparent. Then suddenly everything around them became somber and cold, as shadowy and gloomy as if the season had jumped forward three months in the year, from August to October.

The gorge was a saber cut through the mountain, so deep that the light reached it only for a few minutes every day, when the sun passed across the narrow cleft at its end.

From time to time Therese stopped to give Nendaz time to catch up. Dsozet was walking with him. She could hear Nendaz asking, "How do you feel now?"

"Fine," Dsozet answered.

"How's that hole in your head you got when the mountain fell?"

"That wasn't a hole! It was just a scratch."

"Is it all healed up?"

"Lord, yes! A long time ago."

Therese started off again. She heard nothing more. Then again their voices mounted up to her as they came closer.

"Don't you believe it?" Dsozet was saying.

"Of course not. You're too little."

"Then you won't ask Rebord for me?"

"You wouldn't even know how to use it."

"Me!"

Her love pulled her forward up the mountain. She stopped, she started up again. And Dsozet went on, "Me! You believe that . . . ! We've got one at Premier too. Cattagnoud, the old soldier, has a gun. When I bring him some firewood he lets me borrow it for a little. You ought to see me! I can make sparks with a flint as good as anybody. Only the trouble is you can't shoot Cattagnoud's gun off because the barrel is all warped. So if Rebord would only lend me his. . . . Oh, I'd know how to work it all right! I can pour in the powder and ram it down, and put the bullet in and ram it. . . ."

She could hear Nendaz saying, "What about the recoil?"

"What's that?"

"The kick you get in the shoulder, when you fire a gun off."

"Oh."

" 'Oh' is right! You'd fall right on your backside, you would. How old are you?"

"Fourteen."

"Well, wait until you're twenty."

They had stopped again to catch their breath and all three were sitting down beside the path, leaning back on the grassy slope behind it. Therese said nothing because there was nothing

she wanted to say. It was Dsozet who kept on talking.

"It isn't fair!" he was saying.

"Why isn't it fair?"

"Because Cattagnoud, when I do something for
him . . . And didn't I do you a favor?"

"Well, wait a bit. We'll see."

Then, as they started up again, "You see," said
Dsozet, "there really are some up there in the
rocks. I've seen them myself. They've got their
holes in between the rocks, those marmots have.
And they're smart, too," he went on, "but I know
what I'd do. One of them keeps sitting up in front
of the others for a lookout. And when it sees anybody coming, it whistles. . . ."

He whistled between his fingers.

"But I'm smarter than they are. I've thought it
all out. There are big stones up there you could
hide behind. I'm quick when I want to be, I can
tell you, and I'm nimble too. I can wiggle a long
way flat on my stomach, and I can—"

"Yes, but carrying a gun? They're heavy, you
know. And long, too—longer than you are even."

The light in the gorge was growing stronger.
For some time now they had been getting closer to
the stream. At first it had flowed far down below
them, but the gorge grew shallower as they
climbed, and the bed of the stream rose higher and

higher until finally the tumbling water ran along level with the path. For some time they walked along beside it. Then they saw the first cabin. It stood on the right of the path in a tiny clearing with the spruce forest hanging right over it, reaching far up the steep slope until it gave way in its turn to the towering rocks above.

They walked a little further and saw a second cabin, then three, then four, all of them small and poor-looking.

Her love had brought her this far. The three of them stood on the path. Biollaz was out in front of his cabin. He had seen them coming far down the gorge.

"So you're coming up too, now?" he asked Therese.

"Where is he?" she asked.

Biollaz looked at her silently. He shook his head.

"Look," he said gently, "we're afraid he's kind of lost the use of his wits. It's because of Seraphin —he was your uncle, wasn't he? Well, Antoine keeps insisting he's still alive. He borrowed a pick and a shovel from us, and there was no stopping him. We couldn't do a thing with him. He's gone off to look for Seraphin."

"How about you?" she asked.

"Oh, we don't dare go."

"Why?"

"Why? Well, you see . . . well, that's the way it is . . ."

She said, "We'll have to go up there."

"I tell you," Biollaz protested, "it isn't safe!"

Just then Dionis and the gendarme came down the path from the mountain.

"Nothing to be done!" they said as they came up. "Now he's pretending he can hear his voice."

"Whose voice?"

"Seraphin's. Calling."

"Where?"

"Under the rocks."

"We'll have to go and look for him," Therese said again.

"Look," said the gendarme, "it would be much better for you to wait for him to come down by himself. He'll certainly have to come back sometime, when he's worn himself out. I have to get back, myself, but you could stay right here, and then when he comes down you could speak to him. . . ."

Therese moved forward. She shook her head without answering and started forward again on the path.

Donneloye's wife came out of her house.

"Here you are at last, Dsozet!" she said. "Wherever did you spend the night? Oh, Therese," she said, "Madame Therese, don't go on any further. Come in and stay with me, it will be much better."

Therese didn't seem to hear her.

Then Dsozet's mother called to her son.

"Dsozet, Dsozet!" she called. "Come here! Dsozet, you are not to go a step further!"

And she stood right in the middle of the path, barring his way, so that he had to stop.

But Therese, Therese went by.

And Nendaz and Dionis and Biollaz went with her.

They were still following the stream as it curved around the corner to the left. And there—oh, she could remember it so well, the other times she had come up, the lovely valley opening up as you turned the corner, fresh and green and richly peopled with men and cows! Now in front of her loomed a great boulder, another great boulder, a third. . . . There was a whole wall of enormous stones, like frowning shuttered houses, blocking the path as she looked and seeming to say, "No further."

Between them were only narrow tortured passages, like dark and shadowed alleys. And she would have to plunge into them to go forward, there was no other way. From where they stood they could see the grayish mound of the rest of the landslide looming up behind and above the first rocks, so high that it hid the great plain of stones stretching behind it.

All these things seemed to say to her, "Stop!"

But it had been said to Therese, "Go forward just the same."

Suddenly there he was, in his great cape, his shepherd's crook standing up beside him as high as his shoulder.

He was over on the left, on top of a rock, as still as if he had been carved out of the rock himself. Only his head and his long white beard moved under his wide-brimmed hat.

He stood on their left and a little above them, where the ravine of the Dubonere opens as a deep cleft near the end of the valley.

"Stop!" he called to them.

He looked at Therese.

"Who are you?" he asked. Then he nodded. "Yes, I see. You're Antoine's wife. But are you even sure, woman," he asked her, "if the man you are seeking is still the same as the one you knew?

"They trick people with their false shapes," he said. "They still haven't found rest, and they wander about up there under the stones, jealous of you, envious of you. . . ."

Nendaz, Dionis and Biollaz stopped. But Therese, Therese went on walking forward.

"Woman!" said Plon, "woman, take care. . . . They may look as if they had bodies like us, but it is all trickery. Come and spend a night in my cabin under the cliff if you want to hear them. And see them, too. I've heard and seen them, I have—they're all white, they walk up and down, wailing and lamenting through the night. They make a noise like the wind whistling over the top of a rock, like a pebble rolling around under a stream."

Now it was Therese's turn to stop and stand still. Plon raised his hand to point.

"Do you know what the name of that is, up there? You can see it from where you are. That ridge, I mean, with the place gouged out of it? D. . E. . V. . Oh, he keeps on trying, that one does, and this time he pulled it off."

He nodded his head.

"As for your husband, let him alone, I tell you. He is just as false as any of them. He's only a bit more daring, that's why he came down."

He raised his voice.

"Don't go. If you do, you too will be as lost as they are. Don't let him tempt you up there. The rock pile is full of treacherous holes, full of stones that rock under your feet, it's all ups and downs, and big cracks . . . Don't go, Therese, don't go!"

Therese turned to the men.

"Are you coming?"

"You want to go on?" Nendaz asked.

He looked at her a minute. "Well then," he said finally, "in that case, maybe it would be better if you went on by yourself."

"Very well," she said, "I will go alone."

10

To climb up to Derborence takes seven or eight
hours, when you come from the Vaud country.
The path goes upstream along the banks of a flash-
ing mountain stream. Confined by its steep banks,
the water tumbles downhill like a crowd of heads
and shoulders pushing and jostling each other to
go faster. With shouts and laughter and voices
calling, like a crowd of children just out of school
pushing to get through a narrow door.

You leave behind you the well-built cabins of
those parts, their long low roofs carefully covered
with slates polished by rain and gleaming like bits
of silver. Little brooks pour out everywhere,
brooks as big around as your arm, with such force
that the people use them to turn their churns.

After that, nothing. Nothing but a little cold
wind.

Nothing but a little bit of winter blowing against
your face as you lean over empty space, nothing

but that enormous shadowy chasm below. He was
down there again—but could anyone have seen
him, down there in the very bottom?

No, he was much too small.

Six hundred yards down there he would have
been no more than a tiny white dot, invisible to
the naked eye in the immensity of that stony waste.
In the shadow the rocks were bluish as if they were
perpetually damp, or else a sad gray color with
blackish patches like those you can see on the face
of a corpse.

He was too little and too far away down there
for anybody to see him. And now it seemed that
suddenly the rocks were awake. They looked drier,
they brightened and came to life for a minute. Tipping up suddenly over the ridge, the sun had come
upon them. The man down there at the foot of
those great heaps seemed no bigger than an ant in
the sunlight.

It didn't stop him from lifting his pick, though,
or changing to his shovel to dig again, always trying to find one who was there no longer: poor
Seraphin.

He had no longer the right use of his wits, that
was why he lifted his pick in the sunlight. First he
struck with the pick, then, bending down and gripping the flat shovel by its handle, he dug at a
trench. This was no more than a shallow furrow,

barely showing in the rubble of black schist all mingled with pebbles against which the iron tool struck sometimes, making a clear ringing sound.

And Therese, Therese was at first completely lost in those narrow passages between the biggest blocks of stone. They twisted and turned, more complicated and tangled than any system of village back alleys. Where was she now? Where should she go next? She could barely see the sky, a skein of blue half untangled far above her. Where was south? North? She was completely bewildered, then suddenly the sound of iron striking against something hard and sonorous came to her, saying, "Here he is!"

He lifted his pick and brought it down again; it was as if he was speaking to her from far away.

She stopped. All she had to do now was to listen and make sure where the sound was coming from. She listened and then started off again. She threaded her way around the bottom of first one great mass of rocks and then another. After that the boulders were smaller, packed more closely and piled up on top of each other like stairsteps up which she had to climb—in those wastes where never before had a woman dared venture alone. But she was not alone—for there was love.

He lifted his pick with both hands. He had taken off his coat and vest.

His back was turned to Therese.

He still had on his good white shirt and new trousers; he was there. He looked no bigger than an ant at the foot of the looming pile of rock, but just the same he lifted his pick and brought it down, and then lifted it again.

Therese jumped from one block to a neighboring one, from one shoulder of rock to another shoulder of rock. He heard nothing. He was making too much noise himself. Then he laid down his pick and took up the shovel.

And Therese heard a voice saying, "Go nearer."

The voice spoke again in her heart, "Go forward, keep on, do not be afraid. Don't let him go again. If he runs away, run after him. . . ." She called, he didn't hear.

She called again, "Antoine!"

This time he heard her. He turned around. But when he saw her he began to shake his head. He kept on shaking his head over and over, telling her "No!" and again "No!" and again "No!"

She started forward again. He was saying something, but she couldn't make out what it was. He turned his back, hesitated, then dropped the shovel on the ground. Once more he turned around, saw her still coming, and all of a sudden began to run straight in front of him toward the top of the rock pile.

The men watched from below, but at first they could see nothing.

There were five of them in all: Nendaz, Biollaz and Dionis and two more from Zamperon.

They saw nothing. Finally they sat down on the rocks to wait.

"What should we do now?" one of them wondered.

"There's nothing we can do, any more," they told him. "We'll wait, she'll come down again."

"And Antoine?"

"Oh, Antoine . . . !"

While they talked the sun had come upon them. They were right in the middle of one of the big scallops cut out of the shadow of the range by the sunlight. On their right the shadow lay on the ground in a long needle-like projection, on the left it was all jagged like saw teeth, reflecting the irregular outline of the range behind which the sun travelled on its daily round.

The southern range, directly behind them.

The mountains towered up to the very top of the sky, rising in battlements, in towers, in pointed roofs and steeples, and here and there, as the sun journeyed on behind them, it shone through between the peaks, stretching a long arm down to the valley and bringing with it the lovely golden color of its skin.

212

The two little lakes, not far in front and to the right of the men, gleamed suddenly as the light struck them. They had been sad and lonely, now they looked joyous. The surface of the water came alive and ruffled up lightly as if the sun had dipped a finger in it in passing.

The dark water turned even bluer than the sky and looked as if a silver net had been thrown across it. Between its meshes the men could see a little white cloud moving on the water—leaving the bank, gliding across one lake like a boat, then passing into the other one.

"Hey, look there!"

It was Carrupt. He got to his feet, pointing.

"Don't you see him?"

"Who?"

"Antoine, of course!"

"Where's that?"

"Beyond the big rocks, up there on the slope where the smaller stones are."

"That's right, I can see him."

"Me too," said all of the others.

Antoine was so far away already that he was no more than a tiny white dot on the slope. The color of his trousers blended with the dark patches between the rocks, and all they could see was the little white speck of his shirt. But since it moved, changing its position constantly, they could distinguish it from the other colors on the rock pile, which were motionless and unchanging. He was moving, they could follow his path with their eyes. And they saw that he was moving higher and higher on the rocks, toward the top of the slide and its further reaches by the high cliffs—not toward them.

"Where's he going?"

"Looks as if he's running away."

"That's bad," they said. "He won't come back now."

"And Therese?" they wondered.

"Oh, Therese!" said Nendaz. "She'll surely come back now. What else can she do if he won't listen to her?"

But at that very moment a tiny brownish dot began to move among the rocks, a little below the white one and following it. As one climbed higher, so did the other, as one moved further away from them, the other did too.

Had love been asleep? Now it was awake again.

The men could see both of them clearly in the sunlight, on that slope which seemed from below to be smooth and all in one piece, but when you were closer was really all humps and hollows, cut across with deep cracks and full of holes. He went in front. It was hard for her to follow, but her love sustained her. From time to time she had to help herself with her hands and knees on a steeply inclined rock. At other times they could see her sliding backward as the loose pebbles rolled down under her feet.

"Hadn't we better call her?" they asked each other.

"You call," they said to Nendaz. "You know her better than we do."

"It's too far," Nendaz said.

"Yes, but . . ." they protested, "but . . . you see . . ."

They no longer knew what to say.

Besides, at that very same moment they lost sight of Antoine, and the next minute Therese too had vanished. Both of them had disappeared over the top of the rampart.

A shepherd was caught under the rocks in a landslide. Now he was going back to the rocks as if he could not do without them.

A shepherd disappeared for two months. He came back, then disappeared again. And this time it was even more serious, for he was taking somebody else with him.

The five men were still standing there, and behind them on his rock old Plon waited too. However much they wished to leave, they were held to the spot, for each one of them felt ashamed to make the first move.

And now there was nothing in front of them among the rocks, nothing that moved, nothing alive. There was only Therese's basket which she had set down to have her hands free. The white cloth covering it shone brightly in the sun.

It was then that one of the men began to say something, in so low a voice that it was hard to make it out.

"Maybe old Plon was right after all. Who knows?" he muttered, and the others stirred uneasily.

"Lord save us!" they murmured under their breaths.

"If he were a real man, would he have climbed back up?"

"Lord!"

"Maybe he really is a spirit. And he missed Therese, up there, and came down to get her."

And again came the murmur:

"Lord save us!"

"Just the same," Nendaz said, "we really ought to go up there and see."

"Well," said the others, "have to know first where he's taken her. And what's happened to her there. . . . Besides, it wouldn't do any good anyway. . . ."

And they added, lower still, "If it's what we think it is."

The minutes went slowly by.

They went on standing there, motionless. The sun moved behind a peak and no longer shone on them, but it was still close by, a golden triangle on the ground not far away. The bizarre shapes cut out by the sunlight lengthened, then shrank again into different patterns. The little lakes were once more as dull and gray as sheets of zinc.

It was a game played every day by the changing sun and shadow through the mountain passes. After a while one of the rays of sunlight touched their backs again, and when they felt its warmth on their heads they turned around.

They stared in astonishment.

Not at the sunlight, for that was already leaving them and moving on, and anyway that was all part of the game.

They were astonished at the sight of old Plon. He was getting ready to leave. As they looked at him, standing there behind them in his cape, he shrugged his shoulders, then lifted his shepherd's crook.

And all the flock set itself into motion, moving off together in a single great oval like a ship with old Plon standing at the tiller.

He went off. But then how about us? they

thought. What are we doing here? Plon's had enough of waiting. What are we staying here for?

They turned back for one last look at the mountain. And up there, at the very top of the rock pile, something was moving. First one tiny dot of color seemed to shift against the rocks. Then another. Could it be . . . ?

"Impossible!" they said.

They strained their eyes. They searched the mighty slope where, with the twilight, the shadow mounted inch by inch, eating into the shrinking band of sunlight along the top. They looked again, and soon they had to believe what they saw, for the two dots had moved closer and were side by side. And now they were coming down toward them.

The two dots moved down the mountain, and the shadow rose up along the slope; they went toward the shadow, and the shadow climbed to meet them. And it was really Antoine, and really Therese.

In front of the five men loomed the mountain with its immense walls and towers. The mountain was evil, it was all-powerful, but now one power-less woman had risen up against its might, and had conquered, because she loved, because she was brave. Alive, she had followed life, and had brought back the living one from the midst of the dead.

"Halloa!"

The men gave the call of the mountain between their cupped hands, and from far up on the slope came an answer, for the two up there had called back to them.

They paused for a minute up above as they called. The tiny white dot was motionless against the rocks. Then both the white and the brown started off again, becoming larger and larger as they drew nearer.

Now they could see that the man was helping the woman in the rough places. When a big boulder barred the path he took her in his arms to lift her over.

High up, at the very top of the mountain wall, the glacier streamed with light like a comb of honey. But around the two that were coming— and they were a real man and a real woman—all the valley they were leaving had passed into night and into silence, had become the home of sadness and death forever.

11

DERBORENCE. The name sings softly and a little sadly inside your head as you lean over the great empty space where there is nothing left any more, and it is easy to see that nothing is left.

It is winter down there below you, it is always the dead season there, all the year round. And wherever you look, there is nothing left but stones and more stones and still more stones.

For two hundred years now, more or less.

Once in a long while a flock of sheep wanders through the solitudes, searching for the few blades of grass that grow where the rocks leave a crack for them to spring up. Then the flock drifts here and there like the shadow of a cloud.

Like a cloud shadow darker than the stones around it when the sheep are black, a shadow the same color as the rocks when they are white, and parti-colored if the sheep, as sometimes happens, wear coats of different colors.

As they pass by close at hand their pattering hooves sound like a heavy shower of rain.

As they graze, they sound like the little waves that spring up of an evening in fine weather, lapping against the shore with light, quickly repeated blows.

Through the years, the slow and patient brushwork of the growing moss has colored the biggest boulders bright yellow, gray on gray, and all the shades of green, while their cracks give foothold to many kinds of flowers and ferns and small mountain shrubs with sturdy branches and thick leaves, their glossy berries swaying in the wind like little tinkling bells.